MW00613828

CATFISHED IN CRAIG

An Odds-Are-Good Standalone Romance

New York Times Bestselling Author

KATY REGNERY

Catfished in Craig
Copyright ©2021 by Katharine Gilliam Regnery

Sale of the electronic edition of this book is wholly unauthorized. Except for use in review, the reproduction or utilization of this work in whole or in part, by any means, is forbidden without written permission from the author/publisher.

Katharine Gilliam Regnery, publisher

This book is a work of fiction. Most names, characters, places, and incidents are products of the author's imagination. References to real people or places are used fictitiously.
All rights reserved, including the right to reproduce this book or portions thereof in any form whatsoever.

Please visit my website at www.katyregnery.com

Cover Designer: Marianne Nowicki
Editing: Tessa Shapcott + My Brother's Editor
Formatting: CookieLynn Publishing Services
First Edition: October 2021
Catfished in Craig: a novel / by Katy Regnery—1st ed.
ISBN: 978-1-944810-87-0

In grateful thanks to the amazing coffee shops of
Boston, especially Caffé Nero & The Farmer's Horse;
Ridgefield, especially Starbucks, Bobo's and Tusk & Cup;
and New York City, especially GFG on Beekman and Williams.
xoxoxo

CHAPTER ONE

Tony

LOOKING FOR PARADISE?

SWM, 33, seeks SWF, 21-25.

Let me take care of you.

I'm hot, rich, and single.

You're beautiful, fun, and available.

Join me for island sunsets and walks on the beach.

Let's make memories to last forever.

I didn't choose the town of Craig for its lush, scenic *blah, blah, blah.*

Nor to experience the—*cringe*— "wild frontier of Alaska!"

Nor to "find myself." *Gag.*

The first reason I chose Craig is because that's where my finger landed on the blood-spattered globe that used to sit on my uncle's desk.

The second—and far more important—reason, is because Craig looked like a great place to disappear.

I wasn't wrong.

There are about 1,200 people living in Craig, which is

located on Prince of Wales Island, which is located in the Alexander Archipelago, which is located in the Alaska panhandle. (*Never heard of it? Exactly. Needle, meet haystack.*)

Accessible only by ferry or seaplane, Prince of Wales Island is two hundred twenty miles south of Juneau and fifty-six miles northwest of Ketchikan. Fun fact? The ferry to Ketchikan, which boasts a McDonald's, takes a leisurely three hours.

Three hours for a Big Mac, for crissakes.

Like I said, the perfect place to disappear.

But there's always a trade-off, right? Right.

Now, you might be saying to yourself, "Okay, Tony. No one's ever gonna find you in Craig. But you're in *Alaska*! Cold, snowy Alaska!"

Well, you'd be wrong about that.

Not all parts of Alaska are cold and snowy.

Cool and rainy year-round, with bright, sunny, eighty-degree days in the summer, it's a lot more like San Francisco than how you'd picture "Alaska." Matter of fact, Craig only gets about twenty inches of snowfall a year… which is fine with me. After living the first thirty years of my life in northern New Jersey, I've had enough of "the white stuff" to last a lifetime.

The trade-off, per se, wasn't about the climate or the weather, and even though everything in Craig is pretty damn pricey, that didn't bother me either. I have dough to spend.

The biggest problem in Craig is…

Girls.

Women.

Ladies.

There aren't enough.

There aren't *anywhere near* enough.

Only eight percent of Craig's population is between eighteen to twenty-four years old, and of that paltry eight percent, only forty-four are women.

Over my last three years living in Craig, I'm pretty sure I've met them all, and none of them is—what I'd call—"Tony Material."

My first girlfriend? Back home in Bayonne? Lisa-Marie Cardello. She was named after Elvis Presley's daughter and ten times hotter than Priscilla. At thirteen years old, she had this long, black, glossy hair and lips that could suck the sour out of a lemon. We were together until my freshman year of high school when I dumped her for Dina Gemelli, the daughter of our neighborhood bookie, and hotter than one p.m. on the Fourth of July. After Dina, there was Samantha, and after her, there was Cece. All drop-dead gorgeous.

You get it, right? I'm used to hot girls.

And hot girls have always been into me.

I mean, let's face it—*and I'm not saying this to brag, but facts are facts*—I'm a catch. Tall, dark, and handsome, my hair is wavy and thick, my eyes are dark blue, and my lips are full. When I smile? *Cavolo!* My Zia Marina used to say in her native Sicilian: "Tuo sorriso, Antonio! Mi fa battere il cuore…" My smile made her heart pitter-patter. And she wasn't the only one.

So, not for nothing, but I think I deserve a girl who, well, *matches* with me. Physically. Someone tall, dark and beautiful, with great tits, a tight waist, and a smile that stops traffic. Frankly, this isn't just about *me*, you know? A girl like that? *Madonna!* She *deserves* to be with a looker like me.

So why can't I find her here in Craig?

Well, for starters, Craig ain't Jersey. The pickings are slim, and the women here don't take care of themselves the way they do back at home.

For the most part, they don't give a crap about how they look. Their hair's never done up, and their nails are short and stubby. Some of 'em should probably lay off the sauce. Most of 'em should lay off the french fries.

And the deal breaker?

A *lot* of 'em have kids.

Now, don't get me wrong: I got nothing against kids in general. Hell, I'd like ten of my own someday. I just don't want to raise someone else's brat. No offense.

Like I said: they're just not "Tony Material."

But last week I remembered something my Zia Marina used to say when I was little: "If the mountain can't get to Mohammed, then Mohammed better get his ass over to the mountain."

And that made me think: if I can't find a girl who's "Tony Material" already *here*, I better figure out a way to get her here. Right? Right. I'm not getting any younger, after all. If I want those ten kids, I'm going to have to get started soon.

So, here's what I did: I placed an anonymous personal ad in this magazine called "Odds Are Good." I want someone young, someone fun, and, most importantly, someone beautiful. Just to be safe, I'm not buying her a plane ticket to Ketchikan until I see a picture.

But if all goes well, I'm thinking Craig might be perfect, after all.

My uncle's former associates will never find me here, and as long as I got a hot woman to warm my bed during those twenty inches of snow a year?

Life could be—*bada bing, bada boom!*—a dream.

Yes, indeed.

Life could be a dream, sweetheart!

CHAPTER TWO

Tessa

Pig, I think, reading the short personal ad once, then reading it again. *He's thirty-three years old, and he's looking for a twenty-one-year-old girl? Men. They're all pigs.*

But despite my disgust, my eyes zero in on the fourth line and linger there.

Let me take care of you.

I don't want to like these words, because they're coming out of the mouth of a pig, but I can't help it. I run my finger over the letters, sighing softly.

"Tessa!" calls my cousin, Francesca, from the reception desk. "Can you do a wash and set at four? Please, please, please?"

I look up, shaking my head. "No. I gotta get Gia from daycare."

"Your mother can't get her?" she asks, exasperated.

My mother adores my daughter, but now that my parents are moving back to Italy, my mother's been relentless about my finding backup childcare help. If I ask her to pick up Gia and babysit until five, no doubt she'll get on my case again.

Either that, or we'll get into another round of: "Come home with us to *bella Italia*! We have plenty of space, *cara*, and you can't cope here on your own. A single mother. *Porca miseria!* Besides, Gia will love *Italia*!"

While I'm sure my daughter *would* love Italy, I'm equally certain I would not. I've visited enough to know that the men there are worse chauvinists than… than… —my eyes glance down at the magazine in my hands—than the guy who wrote the stupid ad I keep reading.

"Tessa! Yes or no?" demands Francesca.

"No!" I yell back, my raised voice turning a few gray heads in my direction, rheumy eyes wide and disapproving. "I told'ja already. I gotta get Gia."

"I'm so sorry, Mrs. Fillipi, but Tessa can't take you today," says Francesca, shaking her head at me with disgust. "She's having childcare issues."

It's on the tip of my tongue to say that I'm *not* having childcare issues. I never promised my cousin overtime, and last I checked, seven a.m. to three p.m. is a full, eight-hour day. Besides, I like leaving at three. It's important to me to be on time for Gia.

"Tomorrow at nine? Let me check. Hmm. No, Tessa's booked until one. Can you come at one-fifteen?"

Great, I think. *Fifteen minutes to shovel some food into my mouth tomorrow between appointments. Ain't life a dream.*

"Wonderful. Thank you for being so flexible, Mrs. Fillipi."

Francesca hangs up the phone and runs her long nails through her half-foot high, gelled-to-within-an-inch-of-its-life hairdo. My cousin's style is hopelessly stuck in 1985 and she gives exactly zero shits if you don't like it.

"Before I forget," she says dramatically, turning flinty eyes to me. "Thank *you* for being so flexible, as well, *Theresa*."

I roll my eyes at her use of my full name, but I don't look up from my magazine, and a second later she's distracted by an arriving client, thank Christ.

Savoring the last ten minutes of my break before my final client of the day arrives for a cut and blow-dry, I re-read Mr. Paradise's ad again, bypassing the first few lines and skipping to the part about sunsets, walks on the beach, and good times.

Although I live in New Jersey, which is basically just a giant peninsula surrounded by water, I can't remember the last time I saw a sunset on the beach, took a walk in the sand, or frankly, had a good time with someone of the opposite sex.

Gia's dad was my last significant other, though he insisted on keeping our relationship a secret because—as he once explained—"some girls are perfect in the dark." In other words, I wasn't pretty enough for him to claim publicly as his girlfriend; I was only good enough for him when we were alone in the dark.

And sure, it hurt my feelings, but you gotta understand—Giancarlo was the hottest guy in our high school by a mile, and I was a Little Miss Nobody. Knowing that I could satisfy him behind closed doors *meant* something to me, and I even convinced myself he cared about me, in his own secret way. Part of me may have even gotten off on the fact that we were secret lovers.

But, anyway, I never demanded that he treat me like a girlfriend. I turned a blind eye when he asked a different girl to the school dances, or after high school when I saw him out on the town with one of his various, gorgeous girlfriends. I went along with late-night booty calls and long Sunday mornings tangled up in his sheets because being in his life some of the time was better than not being in his life at all.

When I shared with him, at age twenty-three, that I was pregnant, he'd given me a choice: he'd pay for an abortion, or he'd privately and quietly pay for eighteen years of child support. But under no circumstances did he want to marry me *or* be a daddy to our child. In fact, he went so far as to tell me that he would never acknowledge Gia as his.

Though I was a little disappointed, I wasn't crushed, and I certainly wasn't surprised. After half a dozen years of being his secret sidepiece, I didn't expect him to suddenly propose. Giancarlo D'Angelo had never been "forever" material. Not for plain, pudgy me, anyway. Popular in school, the son of a wealthy businessman and too beautiful for words, Giancarlo was a veritable god in our Italian American section of Newark, what with his family name and connections.

I knew my place in the equation, and I wasn't "girlfriend" material for Giancarlo. Not by a longshot. I wasn't pretty enough, thin enough, or stylish enough, and while my family was respectable, they weren't wealthy or influential enough to make up for my shortcomings. That said? I'm also a staunch, lifelong Catholic. There's no way I was getting rid of my baby, so I settled for being a single mom, and keeping the identity of Gia's dad under lock and key.

For our daughter's sake, I'd originally hoped he'd change his mind about acknowledging her. But as the months went on, and my belly grew bigger and rounder, he sought me out less and less often. It didn't take long for me to give up on the notion of Gia having him as a dad, and that was okay, because he never promised me any different.

And it's important to note that Giancarlo kept his word.

The day Gia was born, a check for two thousand dollars hit my bank account, and another has appeared like clockwork on the first Monday of every month since.

I haven't seen more than a glimpse of Giancarlo since our daughter's birth four years ago, and I've never publicly disclosed the name of her father. I have no reason to shame him and a couple of good reasons to keep quiet.

One, I appreciate the checks. They help with my rent, groceries, healthcare, and Gia's daycare, and mean that I don't need to work overtime for Francesca to make ends meet.

And two, I don't want the senior D'Angelos to find out that Gia is their grandchild. My father always steered clear of the D'Angelo brothers: Giancarlo's father, Santo, and his uncle, Vito.

Santo and Vito D'Angelo, he always told me, *are bad news. They give law-abiding, hardworking Italians a bad name.*

"So!" bellows Francesca, who suddenly appears before me with her hands on her hips. "When're you getting a babysitter, huh?"

"You volunteering?" I ask.

"Ha!" She chortles. "Mine're in middle and high school. Practically self-sufficient. You think I want to go back to diapers? No way."

"Gia's toilet trained, Fran, and you know it."

"God bless sweet Gia," she says, clasping her hands together. "But your kid, your problem."

"You think Rosemarie might be interested in helping me out now and then? Now that Mamma and Pappa are leaving?"

"Not on your life. She's having too much fun being a college girl."

Francesca and Rosemarie Rizzo bookend a family of six sisters with Francesca, the oldest, at forty-three, and Rosemarie, the youngest, at twenty. As their only cousin on their father's side, I land between the two youngest sisters in birth order. I'll be twenty-eight this fall.

"And the rest of the girls are married. Or, you know, almost married," says Francesca, as though it's news to me that five of my six cousins are married or well on their way to the altar, while I have no significant other to speak of, and one bastard child. She clucks softly, pursing her lips in thought. "Wait a sec. You know what? I overheard Anne Marie at the nail salon talking about a nice Jamaican lady who watches her kids now and then. Let me try to get her number."

I sigh softly.

I'm sure she's very nice, but I just don't want someone else looking after my child. While I would welcome the help of family, I really hate the idea of a stranger caring for my baby.

Which leaves me… nowhere.

I don't have any brothers or sisters. My parents are moving away. My mother's family never left Italy, while my father's sister and her daughters already have their hands full. I can either find a babysitter for Gia, or my life will quickly narrow to me and her once my parents leave. I'll work while she's in preschool from seven a.m. to three p.m. and be her mommy every other moment of the day.

While I don't totally hate this notion, I know it's not exactly healthy either. I'll barely ever see my girlfriends, and the chances of my meeting someone will move from slim to none. And the truth is, I'm lonely. I'd *like* to meet someone. I'd like it very much.

Francesca shoves a scrap of paper in my hand, and I dutifully put it in my pocket to throw away later.

"You know," she says, "if you don't want to hire someone to give you a hand, you could always try to find… you know…"

My head snaps up. "A man?"

"Well! Why not?"

"I don't need a man to swoop in and save the day."

"It's obvious you want to stay home with Gia, and a husband could make that happen for you. You could quit working here and let him bring home the bacon. Lots of older guys would love the idea of a ready-made family."

Older guys.

I cringe.

Older guys past their prime, who'd somehow missed the love boat in their twenties, thirties, and forties.

Older guys whose mothers are gone, but who would hold a young wife to the unimpeachable standard of a dead woman.

Older guys set in their ways, who want someone to cook, clean, and lie ass-up for doggie-style every Friday night at nine.

Older guys who are balding, and thick around the middle, and running out of options.

Older guys, who'd be willing to take on a plain-looking, size fourteen, almost twenty-eight-year-old and her four-year-old bastard daughter.

No, thank you.

"I don't want an *older* guy."

"Not to be mean, but beggars can't be choosers," says my sweet cousin matter-of-factly.

"I'm not a beggar. I have a job, my own place, and Gia. I'm doing fine."

"But you're about to lose your support network," she informs me, and she's so high and mighty about it, I wish I could punch her smug face.

Instead, I ignore her, looking back down at my magazine like it's the most fascinating piece of literature in the entire universe. By the grace of God, the salon phone rings, and she hurries back to the desk to answer it, but before she picks up the receiver, she calls over to me:

"Call the Jamaican lady. At least then you can get out once in a while."

Huffing softly, I close my eyes and sit back in the waiting area guest chair, losing myself in the white noise of hairdryers, running water, and neighborhood chitchat. Although I'm loathe to admit it, Francesca's right. I wish I could stay home with Gia every day, finger painting and baking cookies. I'm sad that she has to go to preschool for eight hours a day when many of her peers only go for three or four. Being a stay-at-home mom sounds like… heaven.

Against my will, my mind circles back to Mr. Paradise.

Let me *take care* of you.

Let *me* take care of *you.*

I try the sentence a few different ways in my head, half-hating myself for how much it makes me swoon, not only because I'm positive that Mr. Paradise is a pig, but because I bristle against the notion that I need a man to "take care of me," in the first place.

Not to mention, I'm absolutely, positively not what he's looking for.

Single white female.

Check.

But the rest? Nuh-uh.

Under twenty-five.

Ha.

Beautiful.

Nope.

Fun.

Not anymore.

Available.

Almost never.

I open my eyes and look at the older women sitting in the dated salon chairs, their weekly coifs being sprayed into submission.

Is this where you want to be in twenty years? I ask myself. *Gia will be all grown up by then, and what'll you have to show for your life? No husband. No home. A job you hate, a lonely apartment in downtown Newark, and a child who's probably moved away. You only get one life. Don't you want more?*

Like what? whispers my heart. *Like island sunsets, walks on the beach, and memories to last a lifetime? Like someone who'll "take care" of you?*

Fat chance. I'm not beautiful and I'm not young. Women like me—single moms scraping by on child support and a job at a local salon—don't get island sunsets and romantic walks on the beach. We get early bedtimes and nagging older cousins.

I open the magazine on my lap and look at the ad again, feeling angry.

Hot, rich, and single.

A vision of Giancarlo slides through my head and I wince as I think about the way I settled for being his anonymous fuck buddy and equally anonymous baby-mama. An unfamiliar indignation rises up within me, making my chest ache and my eyes water.

How come average women like me allow beautiful men to get away with crap like that? It's not fair. It's not right. It's not okay.

Slamming the magazine shut, I take it to the garbage can, but just before I toss it in, I flip it open and memorize the contact information for Mr. Paradise.

On behalf of all the plain Janes in the world, jerks like him deserve to be taught a lesson, I think. *And I'm just the girl to teach it.*

CHAPTER THREE

Texts

Chapter 3

Texts

TONY: Thanks for giving me your number. I hate email. Are you sure text is okay?

THERESA: Yeah. Text is way better for talking.

TONY: Can you talk now?

THERESA: Sure. I'm on my lunch break.

TONY: I was hoping. It's 8am here.

THERESA: OMG. That didn't even occur to me. Huge time difference.

TONY: Yeah. It took me a while to get used to it.

THERESA: Why? Where are you from?

TONY: Bayonne.

THERESA: Oh, wow. Close. Small world, huh?

TONY: Yeah. I moved up here a few years ago.

THERESA: I bet there's a story there.

TONY: Maybe I'll tell it to you someday. ☺

THERESA: So, it's almost time for you to go to work, huh?

TONY: I work for myself so I can set my own hours.

THERESA: What do you do?

TONY: I'm a contractor.

THERESA: Oh. Cool. My dad's a plumber.

TONY: Similar. What do you do?

THERESA: I'm a hairdresser. I work at my cousin's salon. Seven to three every day. Eight hours of fun. Not. LOL.

TONY: In Newark?

THERESA: Yeah.

TONY: So, I was wondering if I could ask you something.

THERESA: Go ahead.

TONY: Would you be okay sending me a picture of yourself?

THERESA: …

TONY: I could send one of me to you, too. We could trade pics.

THERESA: Whatever. I don't need a pic.

TONY: For real?

THERESA: Yeah. Looks aren't that important to me.

TONY: Huh. You don't hear that too often.

THERESA: Yeah. Well, I mean, if you're a douche, what do I care if you're cute? I think it's more important to get to know someone on the inside first, don't you?

TONY: …

THERESA: Maybe you don't need a picture of me. Maybe you could decide if you like me based on my personality, not my looks.

TONY: I bet you're hot.

THERESA: What if I'm not? You gonna stop talking to me?

TONY: …

TONY: We could still be friends.

THERESA: ☠

TONY: What does that mean?

THERESA: Toxic. LOL.

TONY: LOL. Um.

THERESA: …

TONY: So, will you send me a pic? Just one little pic?

***

TONY: OMG. I was right! I'm so glad you decided to send me a pic. You're so fucking hot! 🌡

THERESA: You liked that pic, huh?

TONY: Yeah. Your body's amazing.

THERESA: Young and hot. Just how you like them.

TONY: And pretty. You're really pretty. You could be a model if you was taller.

THERESA: Oh, sure. My father would just love that.

TONY: No?

THERESA: Of course NO. What Italian father wants pics of his daughter plastered everywhere, huh?

TONY: LOL! I guess you're right.

THERESA: So now that you've seen a pic of me, I guess you want to keep talking to me, huh?

TONY: Definitely.

THERESA: Just out of curiosity… what if I hadn't been hot? What if I'd been a little chunky? Or a few years older?

TONY: But you are hot. And you're skinny. You look 20. The question's moot.

THERESA: Yeah, but… what if?

TONY: Honestly? If there's no attraction, I don't think a relationship can work.

THERESA: But what if the person is hot, but a terrible person?

TONY: At least I'd have something nice to look at while I found that out.

THERESA: …

TONY: LOL.

THERESA: ...

TONY: Um…you like going to the movies?

THERESA: Sure.

TONY: Since I moved here, that's what I miss the most. Movie theaters.

THERESA: Where are you, exactly? Somewheres in Alaska, right?

TONY: Yeah. I live in Craig. It's a little town on Prince of Wales Island.

THERESA: Is it near, um, what's it called… um, Anchoredge?

TONY: No. Not close. Anchorage is, like, a forty-hour drive north. With a ferry ride. Or two.

THERESA: Oh, wow. So, where the fuck are you anyway? The middle of nowhere, right?

TONY: Sorta. LOL. So, Craig is on an island, right? If you want to leave the island, you have to take a 3-hour ferry or a 30-min flight to Ketchikan. Once you get there, you can take a flight on Alaska Airlines or Delta Airlines to anywhere else.

THERESA: What'd you go there for? To escape the mob? LOL.

TONY: …

TONY: Um.

THERESA: Just kidding. *Sopranos* joke. You know, because I'm from Newark and you're from Bayonne?

TONY: Someone's at the door. I gotta go.

THERESA: Yeah. Okay. Bye.

***

TONY: Hi.

THERESA: Hi. You're back.

TONY: Yeah. How was your day?

THERESA: Good. Fine. You know, same old.

TONY: You said you're a hairdresser, right?

THERESA: Yeah. It's my dream job… not.

TONY: I bet you take real good care of yourself. I mean, I can tell that from your photo.

THERESA: …

TONY: I just mean, your hair is beautiful. ♥

THERESA: Yeah, I get what you meant.

TONY: So, you work for your cousin?

THERESA: Yeah. Francesca.

TONY: LOL. That's such an Italian name.

THERESA: My father's from Naples. Her mom, too. They're brother and sister.

TONY: What about your mom?

THERESA: From Sorrento. So, yeah. I'm Italian. 100%.

TONY: You were born there?

THERESA: No. In Brooklyn.

TONY: Ha! Me too!

THERESA: Get outta here! You're from Brooklyn?

TONY: Born there, yeah. But my grandparents were from Palermo.

THERESA: Oh. You're Sicilian.

TONY: Ethnically, yeah. Both my parents were born in America, but my aunt and uncle raised me from little. My parents were in an accident when I was six and died.

THERESA: Jesus.

TONY: …

THERESA: I'm so sorry. ✞

TONY: That got dark quick, huh? LOL. Sorry.

THERESA: No. I'M SORRY. That's really sad. I didn't expect you to say that.

TONY: It's sad, yeah, but it was a long time ago. My aunt and uncle were good to me.

THERESA: …

TONY: You still there?

THERESA: Yeah. I'm just...I'm really, really sorry.

TONY: Thanks. Um. Subject change! Would it be okay if I sent you some pictures of Craig? Where I live? It's beautiful here. You gotta see it to believe it.
THERESA: Sure. You can send me pictures, I guess.
TONY: Cool. Check your phone in a few minutes.

***

TONY: Haven't heard from you since yesterday. Did you get the pictures I sent?
THERESA: Sorry. I had things to do. Yeah. I got them. It's pretty there. You were right.
TONY: You'd love it.
THERESA: How do you know?
TONY: Because you have good taste.
THERESA: You don't know me well enough to say that.
TONY: You take care of yourself. You're hot. I like the outfit you're wearing in the pic you sent. Good taste. I can see it. I can tell.
THERESA: Not for nothing, but you can't. You don't know me at all.
TONY: You're going to argue with a man calling you gorgeous, Gorgeous? ;)
THERESA: ...
TONY: …
THERESA: …
TONY: Okay. Okay. You have shitty taste. Is that better?
THERESA: LMAO!
TONY: *Now* she smiles?

THERESA: Actually, she laughed.

TONY: Wish I could have heard it.

THERESA: It's nothing to write home about.

TONY: How do you know? You're home. I bet it sounds amazing. Now I miss Jersey.

THERESA: You're in a beautiful place. Why do you miss it here? Your family?

TONY: Nah. No family left in Jersey, really. But I don't know. It'll always be home, I guess. You can't get decent food here. People try to imitate my accent and it's a joke.

THERESA: Not a big *paesan* community in Craig, Alaska, huh?

TONY: My best friend's Irish. ♣

THERESA: Still a Catholic, at least.

TONY: LOL. Yeah. We meet up at St. John by the Sea up in Klawock sometimes for Sunday mass.

THERESA: I like the name of that church. It sounds nice. ☺

TONY: You go to mass, Theresa?

THERESA: What do I want… to go to hell when I die?

TONY: …

THERESA: Of course I go to church!

TONY: LMAO. That was so Jersey.

THERESA: You can take the girl outta Jersey, but you'll never get Jersey outta the girl. LOL!

TONY: You know what? You're fun. ☺

THERESA: Yeah? You are too. Surprisingly.

TONY: Why surprising?

THERESA: You put a lot of importance on looks and age in your ad. I didn't know what your personality would be like.

TONY: Luckily, we're both hot, so we don't have to worry about that.

THERESA: …

TONY: Right?

THERESA: Phone's ringing. I gotta go.

***

TONY: Hey. You around?

THERESA: Yeah. Hi.

TONY: So, I was just wondering… how come you're single?

THERESA: You mean, because I'm so hot and so young and so fun?

TONY: LOL! Yeah. Exactly.

THERESA: Things didn't work out with my last boyfriend. He wasn't into commitment.

TONY: That's weird. I think any guy would be lucky to be with you.

THERESA: …

THERESA: Well, he didn't agree with you, I guess.

TONY: Maybe he just wasn't looking for anything serious.

THERESA: You can say that again.

TONY: Well… maybe his loss can be my gain.

THERESA: How so?

TONY: How would you feel about talking on the phone? I'd like to ask you something…you know, in person.

THERESA: In person? I hate to break it to you, but you're in Alaska and I'm in Newark. In person is impossible, Tony.

TONY: Wiseass.

THERESA: I aim to please. ;)

TONY: You know what I mean. Can I call you or what?

THERESA: Sure.

TONY: How about Saturday?

THERESA: Okay.

TONY: Ten pm your time?

THERESA: I'll be waiting.

CHAPTER FOUR

Tony

Theresa.

My dream girl's name is Theresa.

Born in Brooklyn to Italian parents, she lives in Newark, of all places, not far from where I grew up in Bayonne, across the Newark Bay.

Petite, with a great smile, tiny waist, and perfect tits, she's twenty-two and works as a hairdresser for her cousin. She found my ad in an *Odds Are Good* magazine someone left behind at the salon and liked what I wrote.

When I asked her why she was single, she said things didn't work out with her last boyfriend because he was a commitment-phobe. That doesn't totally track for me, because she seems pretty fun over text, but more importantly, because this girl is hot.

H. O. T.

Scorching hot.

Red hot.

White-hot.

In my late uncle's words, "a stone-cold fox."

With jet black hair and deep brown eyes, she could easily be a model if she was just a little taller. When I told her this, she said—*How cute is this?*—her father wouldn't like it. I fuckin' loved that. She's hot as fuck, but she's no slut, my Theresa.

A Madonna in the body of a siren.

Theresa.

For a week now, I've been listening to the song "Maria" from *West Side Story*, but I substitute the name "Theresa" for "Maria."

♪ *Theresa! I've just met a girl named Theresa!* ♫

Call me corny if you want, but frankly, I can't stop thinking about her.

There is one question that circles endlessly in my head, though: How do I sell Craig to a girl like that?

♪ *And suddenly that name will never be the same to me!* ♫

I'm in the middle of belting my favorite part of the song when my doorbell rings. It's my friend, "Big" Jim Kerrigan, looking for a cold beer and a few hands of gin rummy, our standing Thursday evening game.

"Was that you singing?" he asks, thrusting a six-pack of beer at my chest.

"Yeah. 'Maria' from *West Side Story*. You know it?"

"No." He raises his eyebrows. "You into show tunes, Tony?"

"Nah. My Zia Marina loved that movie," I tell him. "She always had it on. I must've seen it a hundred times."

He follows me into the house, heading to the back deck while I make a detour to the kitchen.

I bought this place for cheap two years ago when I decided to stay in Craig and did all of the updates on it myself. Originally a log cabin design, I took advantage of the harbor views by adding a large deck off the back and replaced the south-facing living room and dining room walls with windows. The kitchen is the best equipped in Craig, and I had all of the fixtures and furniture shipped up from Seattle.

It's considered a "show place" among the locals and quickly got my one-man construction business off the ground. I like to think my uncle Gino is looking down, proud of me for my accomplishments. Once upon a time, in another life, he taught me everything I know.

I gulp over the memory of my late uncle, something awful—that I desperately try to ignore—twisting painfully inside of me.

Taking a sharp breath, I throw the six-pack into the fridge and follow Jim onto the deck. We became fast friends when I started renovating this place: Jim, called "Big Jim" by the locals because he was a high school linebacker and the Gatorade Alaska Football Player of the Year ten years ago, owns a local lumberyard and says I'm his best customer.

I already have two ice-cold bottles of Peroni waiting for us on the picnic table where we play cards. Closing the sliding door behind me, I crack them open and offer one to my friend.

"So?" he asks. "What's got you singing?"

"A girl," I say, clinking my bottle against his.

"Okay, okay! This is news!" He throws back the suds and takes a long sip. "So? Who is she? Mandy? At the pool?"

Craig has a very decent public aquatic center where I

swim a few times a week, and Mandy's a not-awful-looking lifeguard there. She's thin, with long blonde hair, but she has what my *Zia* would have called a "horse face."

"Nah," I say, taking a seat at the table and shuffling the deck of cards like a Vegas dealer. "Been there. Done that. No thanks."

"Rachel Morehouse?" he asks, staring down at the table. He's referring to the art teacher at the local elementary school who I dated for a few weeks last year.

I shake my head. "Nah. Not Rachel either."

"Phew," murmurs Jim.

Interesting. I didn't realize he liked her.

"What gives?" I ask him. "You like Rachel? Why haven't you asked her out?"

Jim's cheeks pinken under his red bushy beard. "How do you know I haven't?"

"Oh yeah?" I ask, dealing us each a hand. "And what? She turned your ugly Irish ass down or what?"

"Nah. I was bluffing." He shrugs, picking up his cards. His beefy fingers make them into a messy fan. "I haven't asked her out yet. Still working up my courage. She's… well, you know."

I *do* know.

Mandy and Rachel are the best of the bunch in Craig, with Rachel edging out Mandy in both looks and personality. They're both single, without kids, and still in their early twenties—nice enough girls who aren't too fat, too ugly, or too annoying.

That said? Horsey Mandy doesn't have a whole lot

going on upstairs, and Rachel, who's petite with short, reddish-blonde hair and bright green eyes, lives with and cares for her aging, sickly, permanently-in-a-shitty-mood father. Not a whole lot of opportunity for private time, if you know what I mean; not to mention, old man Morehouse ain't exactly a selling point. Still, when you're the best catch in a town where men outnumber women by a good margin, every single guy around eventually has you on his radar. So, yeah. I know Rachel.

"You better move fast," I say, neatly dropping a pair of kings to the table and taking two new cards from the deck. "She's gonna get snapped up quick."

"Yeah. Yeah. I know." Jim sighs heavily, taking a card and placing it into his fan. "Enough about me. What about you? Who's Maria?"

"Nah. Maria's the name of the girl in the song. My girl? Her name's *Theresa*."

"Theresa, huh? Don't know her. She just move here?"

I shake my head, picking a card, then laying down a pair of aces. "Nah. She's from back home."

"Joisey?" he says, raising his eyebrows at me.

Jim thinks he knows how to talk like me, but he don't. It doesn't matter how many reruns of *Jersey Shore* he watches. No one can nail a Jersey accent except someone from Jersey.

"Ha. Nice try. Amateur," I say, watching him lay down three threes.

"Old flame?" he asks.

"*New* flame."

"Someone from back home set you up over email or

something?"

"Nah," I say, picking a new card. "I put an ad in a magazine looking for a girl. Asked the circulation department to target advertising to the New York metro area. So, you *could* say, she found me."

"A personal ad," says Jim, staring at his cards and stroking his beard. "That's risky."

"You think?"

"Hell, yeah." Jim picks up two cards and lays down a single ace on my aces. "What if you fall totally in love with her and then find out she's…"

"She's what?"

Jim shrugs, looking up at me. "Not your type."

"Ugly?"

"Or fat. Or annoying. Or fifty-five years old. Or… fuck: a dude!"

"I'm way ahead of you," I tell him, drawing two cards and laying down three queens. "I made her send me a picture… and she's the hottest chick I have ever seen."

"Okay. Fair enough. But how do you *know* it's really her?"

I stare back at Jim, processing his question.

"Have you FaceTimed?" he asks.

"She has an Android."

"Skyped?"

"Who uses Skype anymore?"

"Zoomed?"

"Everyone's sick to death of Zoom after the pandemic."

"Have you even talked to her on the phone?"

"We're talking this weekend."

He raises his eyebrows and gives me a look that makes me frown. I hate to say it, but he has a good point. How do I know for sure she looks like her picture? What if she found the picture on the internet and is just using it to reel me in?

"I could ask her to send me a copy of her driver's license," I tell him.

"Now you're using your head," he says, fanning out two jacks on the table. "Just make sure she is who she says she is. You don't want to get catfished."

"Catfished? I never heard of that."

"You know… like those guys on the MTV show?"

"No. What's catfished?"

"I can't believe you don't know this," he says, shaking his head at me. "A 'catfish' is someone who goes online and makes a fake profile with a fake name, fake picture, and fake information. So you think you're talking to this hot supermodel, but you're actually talking to some hobbit with a beard who lives in his parents' basement."

"A catfish," I murmur, staring at him in half-horror, half-disbelief. "Why would someone do that?"

"Who knows?" Jim shrugs. "For attention? For shits and giggles?"

"Fuck."

"Yeah. It's a real thing, and you" —he points at me with a stern expression— "need to beware."

I nod at him. "Yeah. Yeah. I will. For sure. I'll get her to send a picture of that license. Tomorrow."

Maybe tonight.

Jim places a queen on my trio and gives me a shit-eating grin, but I couldn't care less. Until I see proof that Theresa is who she says she is, nothing else matters.

***

Screw Big Jim.

Catfished.

Fuhgeddaboudit.

I'm staring at a scanned copy of Theresa's driver's license on my computer screen, the ID number blacked out because my girl's no dummy, reassured yet again that my fears were unfounded. She's just as gorgeous on her license as she was in the photo she sent. And there's her birthdate and address, too. She's honest, my Theresa. I never had anything to worry about.

That said, I'm getting tired of singing "~~Mar~~Theresa," without a solid plan to meet her. Since today's our first phone date, I've decided to ask her to come visit me in Craig. No point in waiting any longer. She's gorgeous. She's fun. She's smart. She's perfect for me.

If I want this to go anywhere real, we need to meet. In person.

Being the gentleman that I am, I'm going to offer to pay for her ticket from Newark to Ketchikan; in fact, to show her how serious I am, I put a thousand dollars on an Alaskan Airlines gift card in her name. I'm planning to email it to her the second she accepts my invitation.

A little nervous before our call, I shower and put on after-shave like we're going out on a real date. I pour myself a glass of Italian Chianti and take a seat on my deck, telling myself to calm down before she calls. The late afternoon September sun is warm on my face and makes the harbor glisten like it's painted with yellow gold. A woman could fall in love with a place like this, couldn't she? God, I hope so.

When my phone rings, I jump, feeling excited and nervous at the same time.

"Hello?"

"Tony?"

"Theresa?"

"Yeah," she says. "It's me."

Her accent is sharper than mine and makes me instantly homesick, which is dumb because there's no one left for me in Bayonne now. My three cousins are spread out between Boston and Miami, and my Zia Marina moved to Boca to live with my cousin, Lena, after my uncle's funeral. But I guess, on some visceral level, Jersey will *always* be home to me.

"Wow. Yeah," I say, laughing softly. "It's you."

"Who'd you think it'd be?"

Ha. Spoken like a true Jersey girl with a little attitude. A little sass. She feels instantly familiar to me, and I love it.

"You sound good," I tell her. "Beautiful."

"Yeah," she says. "You, too. Hot, rich, and single, right? Like the ad said?"

"You got it," I tell her.

"I sure do," she says, a slight edge to her voice.

Is she tired? It's late there. *Maybe she's tired.*

"What time is it there? Like… ten?"

"Yeah," she says. "Ten on the dot."

"And you're an early riser," I say, remembering what she said about working from seven to three every day.

"Uh-huh."

We're silent for a second, which makes me panic. I don't want her to think I'm boring. *Say something. Give her a compliment.*

"So… it's good to hear your voice, you know? You're so gorgeous, Theresa. You really *could* be a model," I tell her.

"Yeah. Okay. Looks are *really* important to you, huh?"

There's that edge again. *Huh. Doesn't she like being flattered?*

"Anyone who says looks don't matter is lying," I tell her, trying to make it sound like a joke, but it comes off as serious instead. I rush to add, "But it's not *everything*, you know?"

"Oh, yeah? So, what else matters to you, huh?"

"A good personality doesn't suck," I say. "Being a hard worker is, you know, a good thing. You seem like a hard worker."

"Yeah, I am," she says. "What else?"

"Family," I say, not that I've got much left. But maybe that's exactly what makes it so precious to me.

"Yeah," she says, her voice slightly warmer. "Family's important. I agree," she adds softly. "I'm really sorry about your parents, Tony."

We're getting too deep, too quick. *Shit.* I don't want that. I don't want her to think of me as some sad-sack orphan.

Lighten it up, I tell myself.

"Yeah, thanks. It is what it is. Back to your question, though… being in good shape is important," I tell her, thinking of her tight body. "And having some style. A sense of style, you know? Taking care of yourself."

"Here we go... back to looks again."

She sighs like she's annoyed.

Shit. I'm fucking this up.

"No," I say, trying to backtrack a little. I forgot what a minefield Jersey girls can be. I'm off my game and need to step it up. "I mean, uh… being healthy, you know? Exercising. Like, running or something."

"You do a lot of running, Tony?"

"I swim," I tell her.

"Oh." She sounds surprised. "Me too, actually. I *love* swimming."

There we go, I think, grinning with relief as her voice warms up again.

"Yeah?" I ask her. "You go down the shore?"

"Nah. I take my dau—*cousin's* daughter to the pool every Saturday morning."

"Oh, yeah?"

"Uh-huh. She's a little fish. She loves the water."

"So, you like kids, huh?"

"Sure," she says. "Love 'em. Who doesn't?"

"You *want* kids?" I dare to ask.

"Of course," she says. "You?"

"Uh-huh," I say, cradling the phone against my shoulder and dreaming about the beautiful babies Theresa and I might have someday. "My own."

"Wait. What?"

"My own," I repeat. "My *own* kids."

"What does *that* mean?" she asks, that edge creeping back into her voice.

"Nothing. I just—you know, I don't wanna raise someone else's kid, you know? I don't want that baggage."

I think she mutters "Shit," but it's so quiet I'm not sure. There's a long, awkward pause until I finally hear her sigh. I'm pretty sure I recognize the sound from my cousins and aunt. It's the sound of a woman about to throw a tantrum.

"Tony? I gotta say something here."

"Oh, yeah?" I grimace at her tone. *Fuck. This is going nowhere good fast.* "Whassup?"

"Stop talking and listen," she demands, and I'm so startled by the fury in her voice, I instantly comply. "I really only called to tell you one thing, and it's this: You're *shallow*, Tony. You're a shallow person. I had you pegged the second I read your ad, but I decided not to be so judgmental. Trade some texts with him, I told myself. Give him the benefit of the doubt. But you know what? My original assessment was a hundred percent correct. You're rich and good-looking and you feel like any girl should be grateful to land you, like you're some giant fucking prize. And you know what? It stinks. *You* stink."

Indignation rises up within me, and I find my voice again. "Now, wait a sec—"

"No! You wait!" she yells. "Open your eyes! There are plenty of nice girls who aren't as hot as… as… as *me*. And maybe they have kids and maybe they have baggage and maybe they didn't have the money for braces and maybe they can't afford Gucci and maybe, *just maybe*, they're just doing their best. Their. Very. Fucking. Best. And then you come along and place an ad like that, and you make them all feel like shit. Like total and complete shit. What right do you have to—"

"Whoa!" I bellow. "Hold up! You don't *know* me, Theresa!"

"Fuck, yes, I do!" she insists. "I know you! I've known guys like you all my life, and I just—I just—you know what? You're *not* a good person, Tony. And you know what else? You don't *deserve* someone like me!"

I clench the deck railing with both hands, my heart racing, my breath coming and going in shallow puffs.

I did *not* see this coming.

I'm flabbergasted.

I'm stunned.

I'm pissed.

Who the *hell* does she think she is?

Where did all of this come from?

We've been chatting over email and text for a week, and I never saw an inkling of this fury. I feel… blindsided. Betrayed. Punctured. I'm deflating like a leaky balloon zooming around the sky in a final death throe, getting smaller and smaller until it drops to the ground; a wrinkled, empty sac on the pavement.

Fuck!

I've been catfished.

"Wow," I mutter. "This sucks. I thought you were—"

"*You* suck," she says softly. "I'm doing a service to every female in the world by telling you what you are! And, by the way, you have *no idea* who I am. None!"

"If that's the way you feel, I guess we should hang up," I say.

"I guess we should," she snaps.

I blink out at the water. The letdown I feel is so crushing, I don't trust myself not to cry. To *cry*, for fuck's sake. I just wanted this to work out. I just wanted a little bit of home up here in Alaska with me and I thought… I really thought…

"So, bye, then," she says, but she doesn't hang up right away. I glance at my phone to see the seconds still ticking by like they don't realize I just got my ass handed to me.

"Well, uh… take care of yourself," I say, my chest still rising and falling rapidly.

"Yeah," she says softly, her voice slightly gentler. "I'm… I mean, I'm… I'm not *sorry*, but you can, you know, do better, Tony. Do better next time. With the next girl."

"Okay," I whisper, still in a daze from her rage, still trying to process what the fuck just happened.

"Bye," she says, her voice thin, like maybe she's on the verge of tears, too. "Take care of yourself."

"Yeah. You, too. Bye," I say, lowering the phone from my ear and pressing End.

After the call disconnects, I fist the phone in my hand and look out at the tarnished gold of the harbor, feeling so fucking sad and lonely, it takes my breath away.

CHAPTER FIVE

Tessa

I thought that would feel… better.

I was *positive* it would make me feel better.

But mostly, I feel like a piece of shit who just threw a sack of puppies in a river to drown. Instead of vanquishing all the plain Janes of the world, I just beat the crap out of some guy who yes, is a shallow, chauvinistic asshole, but probably didn't deserve quite that much hate from me.

It wasn't fair, whispers my heart.

Shut up, my head yells back. *He deserved it.*

But did he?

And if he did, why am I feeling so bad?

When I first answered his ad and he wrote back to me, my mission was rock solid: to reel him in like a fish on a hook, then cut the line when he least expected it, leaving the painful hook embedded in his cheek while he fell.

But over the last week, as we got to know each other a little over email and text, I warmed up to him without meaning to. I looked forward to his messages. He was good-looking and funny and sent me pictures of his beautiful island in Alaska. I was touched by the fact that he was orphaned so early in his life and had somehow made the best of it. He made me laugh out loud more than once with anecdotes about being a fish-out-of-water so far from home, and although he hadn't directly told me why he ended up there, it was a story I was dying to hear.

Now, I never would.

I don't wanna raise someone else's kid. I don't want that baggage.

It pinches my heart and makes me wince. *Baggage. My precious Gia.*

My eyes narrow.

He was *exactly* like Giancarlo: beautiful, ruthless, and as shallow as a puddle.

He deserved every word you said, my brain insists, and while I don't totally believe her, I want to. I *wish* I did.

I'm leaning against the kitchen counter, uncomfortably conflicted and deep in thought, when I hear a small voice ask:

"Mamma? Who you yell at?"

My head snaps up to see Gia standing in the doorway of our living room. She's wearing Sleeping Beauty pajamas and matching slippers. In one hand she clutches her blankie, and in the other, her beloved teddy bear, Urso. He showed up on our doorstep on her first birthday wearing a red collar with a tag bearing his name, but without a note or explanation. I figured it couldn't hurt to give the bear to her. It wasn't like I could afford a hundred presents on my salary. Urso and Gia were rarely apart now—he was her favorite stuffed animal, and she couldn't go to preschool or fall asleep without him.

"Yell?" I ask, crossing the living room in two strides and swooping her up in my arms. I kiss the tip of her nose and give her a reassuring smile. "Mamma wasn't yelling, baby. That was the TV."

She glances doubtfully at the empty, black screen and gives me a look that reminds me so much of Giancarlo, it fists my heart.

"What?" I ask, calling her bluff. "I turned it off! Too much yelling for Mamma, too!"

She rests her dark curly head of hair on my shoulder. "I tired, Mamma."

My heart unfurls like a flower. "Then let's get you back to bed, baby."

No matter what happened between me and Giancarlo, or how he treated me, I will always be grateful for the tiny, perfect human I'm holding in my arms. I can hate the way Giancarlo treated me on one hand, but on the other, I feel this deep wellspring of gratitude for what he gave me and the financial support he still provides. As much as I want to loathe him, it isn't that easy. Nothing in life is black and white.

...which forces me to admit, as I take Gia back to her bed, that I made a mistake with Tony.

No human being can be boiled down to a simple caricature, and it's pretty shitty to do that to someone. Yes, on one hand, Tony was shallow and consumed by beauty, but on the other, he was funny and interesting, and probably had layers I never allowed myself to see. In a rush to vent my fury over Giancarlo, I struck out at an unsuspecting and undeserving target.

It *wasn't* fair. That's why I feel like shit about it.

"*Buona notte, cara mia,*" I tell my daughter, brushing a soft kiss on her forehead and pulling the door closed behind me.

I make my way to my own empty bed with a heavy heart.

What's done is done. God willing, the next woman he meets will be kinder than me, I think, crawling under the covers with a heavy sigh. *And maybe he'll do better with her.*

As for me? If the next guy I meet is a cocky so-and-so, I promise *I'll* do better. Instead of trying to teach him a lesson, I'll offer him an education instead.

***

"Holy shit!"

I look up from Mrs. Barbieri's weekly wash and set. Francesca is on the phone with her mother and her face has gone white.

"Are you sure?" she demands. "*Dio mio, Mamma!* What is this world coming to?"

Most of the salon employees have stopped what we're doing, all eyes fixed on my cousin, who's shaking her head in dismay. She looks up at us, biting her top lip, tears filling her eyes.

"I gotta go, Mamma. Yeah. Yeah. I know. Okay. Yeah. I'll tell the girls here. Send my sympathies, yeah? *Ciao, Mamma.*"

She places the phone on the desk, swipes at her eyes, and takes a deep breath before looking up at us.

"I have some—some very bad news. The police just found the body of Giancarlo D'Angelo," she says, blinking back tears. "He was shot in the back of the head."

The world spins.

Spins wildly.

Madly.

Maniacally.

Like a carnival ride from a nightmare.

"W-What?" I hear myself stutter, the comb I'm holding dropping to the ground with a soft clatter.

"Giancarlo!" she sobs. "Giancarlo D'Angelo. *Dio mio*, his poor mother! He's dead. He was k-killed. Shot. Murdered!"

Murdered.

The word ricochets around in my head like a bullet in an empty keg.

Murderedmurderedmurdered.

There's chatter around me, but it's muted, like I'm underwater, or they're all very far away:

Giancarlo!

That handsome boy!

His poor parents!

This world is full of animals!

My knees buckle and I reach for the chair in front of me to steady myself.

Murdered.

Giancarlo's dead.

My daughter's father is dead.

"What… w-what happened?" I murmur, looking up at

Francesca.

"I don't know any more than what I just said." Her eyebrows furrow at me. "You okay, Tessa?"

I throw up into my mouth.

"I'm… I'm going to be sick," I tell her, turning my head away from Mrs. Barbieri just in time to evacuate my stomach onto the salon floor with a loud splash. "Oh… Oh, my God. I'm s-sorry. Oh, no."

Francesca rushes over to me with a shriek, shoving the reception desk garbage can under my chin. The smell of rotting banana mixed with nail polish remover makes me retch again and my breakfast joins my lunch.

"Jesus, Tessa!" says Francesca, averting her head from the garbage can she's still holding. "It's not like you knew him that well!"

If she only knew.

"We were… in school together," I mutter, nodding at my coworker gratefully when she offers me a wad of tissues and a plastic cup of water. "Same grade."

I wipe my mouth and toss the tissues into the trash on top of my vomit. The water is cool on the back of my burning throat.

"You better now?" asks Francesca, placing a tentative hand on my shoulder.

"Yeah," I say, taking a deep breath. "Sorry. I'll be okay now."

My cousin nods, but there's a glint in her eyes, like she's been presented with a puzzle that needs solving. "I forgot you two were in the same grade. He was such a handsome kid."

Averting my eyes from hers, I swallow another gulp of cold water and nod. "Yeah. Yeah, he was."

"I'll mop up," she says, pulling the plastic liner from the garbage can and gagging as she ties a knot in the top. "Take this out to the dumpster, huh?"

I nod, taking the bag from her.

As I step toward the door, Francesca announces: "The funeral mass is on Friday, ladies. We'll close at two so everyone can go home and freshen up before it starts."

There's a general hum of agreement behind me, but I'm already pushing open the front door and breathing in big gulps of fresh air. As I make my way down the side alley and toss the plastic bag into the bright green dumpster, I realize it bears the sticker "D'Angelo Sanitation Services." The angel-winged logo blurs from my tears.

Whatever dreams I may have had about Gia knowing her father someday were now as dead as he was.

I lean against the brick wall of the alley and weep.

***

The turnout at the church is overwhelming, with every Italian-American family in northern New Jersey, and many relatives from the "old country," turning out to pay their respects to Elena and Santo D'Angelo, who sit alone in the front row of St. Elizabeth Seton church.

Because my parents left for Italy last week, and I still don't have a babysitter, I have no choice but to bring Gia to the funeral with me. We sit in the last pew on the right, Gia suitably dressed in navy blue, since my mother always told me it's not appropriate for children to wear black to a funeral.

I'm uneasy bringing her here on one hand, because my family has always steered clear of the D'Angelos. But on the other hand, it's her father's funeral. I feel like she has a right to be here. Besides, I reason, Giancarlo kept us a secret; his family has no idea Gia exists. And if we sit in the back and leave quickly at the end, we can probably come and go totally undetected.

Giancarlo's cousin chokes up when she gives the eulogy, expressing how close they were as children, praising his protective nature and extolling the warmth of his hugs.

I remember those hugs well, and my eyes, which haven't been dry in days, well up yet again, my own memories assaulting me. Whoever Giancarlo was in this life, he didn't deserve to die in the Pine Barrens with a bullet to the back of the head.

The priest blesses the casket and a stony-faced cadre of six young men lift Giancarlo's body onto their shoulders, solemnly parading him down the middle aisle of the sanctuary and down the stairs of St. Elizabeth's to a waiting hearse.

I expect Elena and Santo D'Angelo to join the casket in the hearse, so I'm surprised to find them receiving guests at the top of the church steps. Holding Gia's hand tightly, I keep my eyes down and try to blend in with the crowd.

With a veil of thick black lace covering her face, Elena D'Angelo shakes hands with people as we exit the sanctuary, barely looking up as we share our condolences with her.

Santo's eyes, however, are sharper, scanning each person's face as if actively trying to find his son's killer. The police have no leads, but most of us know this murder wasn't random.

A capo in the Luciano crime family, Santo is a "made" man with more than a hundred New Jersey soldiers taking orders from him. It was common knowledge that he was grooming Giancarlo, his only son, to take over his territory one day. Apparently, someone wasn't a fan of Santo's plan… and ended it by ending Giancarlo's life.

"*Mi dispiace*," I tell Elena, gently shaking her limp, birdlike hand.

"*Grazie*," she murmurs lifelessly, appearing on the verge of a breakdown. My heart goes out to her. I can only imagine what she's suffering, her only child taken from her so brutally.

Side-stepping to Santo, I take his outstretched hand in mine.

"*Mi dispiace, signore.*"

Santo blinks at me, his blood-shot eyes taking a moment to focus on mine. "*Grazie…*"

"Uh, Theresa. Theresa Rinaldi."

"Rinaldi. Yeah," he says, nodding at me, his eyes narrowing just slightly. "Cosimo Rinaldi's daughter."

I'm surprised he knows my father's name. "Uh-huh. Yeah. My parents moved back to Naples, but they send their condolences."

"Thanks for coming."

He nods curtly, glancing at my hand as he releases it.

Then, suddenly, his eyes slide across my body to my opposite hand, which holds on tightly to Gia's. He stares at her for a second, a muscle in his jaw twitching before his head snaps up.

"Who's this?"

"Oh. My, um… my daughter, Gia." I squeeze her hand. "*Cara mia*, can you say hello to Mr. D'Angelo?"

Gia looks up at her biological grandfather, her amber eyes clear and wide, striking in the afternoon sun. "Hi."

Santo scans my daughter's face, his own eyes widening, his lips parting in surprise. He glances up at me before looking back down at his granddaughter.

"Her… eyes," he murmurs.

…are the exact same color as her father's.

Shit. Fuck.

We need to get out of here.

"I'm sorry, again, *signore*," I say, tugging Gia's hand toward the steps.

But Santo squats down, his face at eye-level with Gia's. He gestures to her bear, and I can hear a soft sob escape his throat. "Who's… who's this?"

"Urso," Gia and Santo whisper at the exact same time.

"Hey!" says Gia, a dazzling smile taking over her beautiful little face. "How did *you* know my bear's name?"

"I met your bear," says Santo softly, reaching out to adjust Urso's collar. "A long time ago. I knew the little boy he used to belong to."

I gulp, panic making my throat tight.

"We're h-holding up the line," I say, pulling Gia closer

to me. "Come on, sweetheart. We have to go."

Santo stands up to his full height, nailing me with a razor-sharp look that stops me in my tracks. "Come to the house tonight."

"For the wake?" I clarify. "Oh. No, sir. *Signore*. We couldn't—"

He leans forward, placing a strong palm on my shoulder, his lips close to my ear. "I'm not asking, Theresa. Be there. In one hour. We need to talk."

I blink furiously, fear filling my chest and making it hard to breathe. "I can't, um.."

"I *insist*," he growls, his voice low and threatening, his breath hot on the shell of my ear.

"Y-Yes. Okay."

Santo leans away, nodding at me before lowering his glance to my daughter.

"I'll see you soon, *bambina mia*," he tells her.

"Okay!" says Gia, grinning up at him and making Urso's paw wave goodbye.

We hurry down the steps of the church, half-running down the street to the safety of our apartment. As I lock the door behind us, Gia runs to her room to play. I lean against the door, panting with exertion.

Santo and Vito D'Angelo are bad news. My father's warning echoes in my head, and I clench my eyes shut, every muscle bunching with fear as I consider what to do.

How could you be so stupid?

How did it never occur to you that Giancarlo might have left that bear for Gia on her first birthday? my brain demands.

Because he wanted nothing to do with her! my heart screams back.

Shit. Shit. Shit!

Now Santo knows that Gia's his granddaughter. And my strong maternal intuition tells me he'll stop at nothing to claim her—to assure her place in his life, in his world.

The same world that just *killed* his son.

I want no part of it.

"We need to leave," I whisper, opening my eyes.

I rush to the back of the apartment, dragging two suitcases out of my closet and throwing them on the bed. I reach into my closet and grab a handful of clothes, tossing them into one of the suitcases, hangers and all.

"Where should we go?" I mutter, upending my lingerie and pajama drawers into the suitcase.

To Mamma and Pappa, I think. *To Italy*.

Except that the number of out-of-town guests at today's funeral attests to the fact that the long arm of the D'Angelo's influence extends to "the old country."

"Where?" I whisper, feeling more frantic each passing second. "Where? Where? Where? Where can I keep her safe?"

Sitting down on the edge of my bed, I open the map app on my iPhone, my finger sliding across the United States until I'm staring at Seattle. It's about as far as I can get without leaving the continental U.S.

Why stop there?

Sliding my finger a little farther left, I blink at the archipelago of islands off Alaska's southern coast, remembering Tony's description of Craig.

Only accessible by seaplane or boat, and three hours from Ketchikan by ferry.

The, *literal*, middle of nowhere.

I feel a rush of relief combined with adrenaline as I toss my passport, a pair of boots, and a winter coat into the suitcase, sitting on it to make it close.

"Hey, baby!" I call to Gia, dragging the second suitcase into her room and emptying her drawers into it. "You and Mamma are going on a vacation!"

"Yippee!" she cries, dancing around the room.

And I know *exactly* where we're going.

CHAPTER SIX

Tessa

I pay for our Alaska Air tickets, which cost $650 one-way, with the $1260 in tip money I've been saving to take Gia to Disney World next year. If I leave a paper trail with credit card receipts, it'll be easier for the D'Angelos to track me down, and I intend to stay hidden. At least until Gia turns eighteen.

Sitting at our gate, I'm as twitchy as a turkey the week before Thanksgiving. It's only once we're off the ground and safely in the sky that I can finally breathe a sigh of relief.

We escaped.

As Gia curls up in the seat beside me and falls asleep, however, my moment of peace is stolen by a giant, new question dominating my mind:

Now what?

Now what, Tessa?

Instead of trying to tackle the hugeness of that question, I concentrate on our immediate plan: we're westbound on a plane headed to Seattle, where we'll land around nine. From there, we'll board a plane to Juneau, where we'll arrive around midnight. Seven hours later, we'll depart for Ketchikan. Once in Ketchikan, we'll take a taxi from the airport to the harbor and board the ferry to Prince of Wales Island, landing in Hollis, Alaska, three hours later. And from Hollis, which is on the east side of the island, we'll have a forty-five-minute ride to the westernmost point, Craig, provided we can find someone to take us.

We should arrive in Craig around one p.m. local time, exactly twenty-seven hours from the time we left our apartment in Newark. Twenty-seven hours in transit.

Middle of nowhere? No shit.

Once I arrive in Craig, I'll need to find someplace for us to stay, and then I can figure out the *bigger* picture of "what happens next." For now, I'm just trying to get us to safety, and safety means putting as much distance between us and Jersey as possible.

Doing some quick math, I calculate that after paying for the taxi from my apartment, our airline tickets, a hot dog and apple juice for Gia at Newark Airport, breakfast in Juneau, a taxi to the ferry in Ketchikan, two one-way ferry tickets to Hollis, and a ride to Craig, I'll have about four hundred fifty dollars to my name. So, finding somewhere to stay is going to be my first big challenge. Some Google research uncovered three hotels, a couple of cabins for rent and bed and breakfast in Craig, but they all cost about a hundred dollars a night. Without an immediate way to make money and my credit cards cut up into little pieces in a Terminal A bathroom, I can only afford four nights of lodging before Gia and I are homeless and broke…

…unless I could find somewhere to stay for free.

Now that would be a game changer. With four hundred fifty dollars in cash, I could feed us for a couple of weeks, while I found a job for me and childcare for Gia. If we ate a lot of peanut butter and jelly, I think it would be enough to get us up on our feet.

...if only we knew someone in Craig.

I bite my lower lip, thinking about my one and only phone conversation with Tony, then wincing at my reflection in the plane window. Though it took place almost two weeks ago, the details of our chat are as fresh—and as cringeworthy—as ever. I baited and attacked a man I barely knew. I went out of my way to contact him, lied to him to make myself as appealing as possible, doctored my driver's license with my cousin Rosemarie's photo to make him want me… and then—without warning—I verbally gutted him.

If I were Tony? I wouldn't want anything to do with me.

In fact, if I were Tony, and there was an opportunity to *hurt* me? I might go out of my way to make it happen.

Maybe Craig isn't the smartest plan, after all.

Then again, I look at the curly black hair resting on my thigh and my heart swells with love. I have to protect her. I will do *anything* to keep her safe. And if that means traveling to the ends of the earth and making amends to the only soul I know there? So be it. That's what I'll do.

My apology to Tony needs to be epic. Beyond epic.

My apology needs to be *legendary*.

***

In my entire life, I think, looking out the window at the scenery on Prince of Wales Island, *I have never been this weary.*

Gia, on the other hand, slept four hours on the flight to Seattle, two hours on the flight to Juneau, and five hours on my lap in the Juneau Airport. She's fresh as a daisy.

"You got bears here, Mr. Tom?"

We met Tom Webster and his wife, Mildred, on the ferry from Ketchikan to Hollis. Returning home to Craig after visiting their daughter and granddaughters in Seattle, they were immediately taken with Gia, and she with them. When I asked if they could suggest someone in Hollis who could give us a ride to Craig, Tom insisted on driving us himself.

"Our car's below in the hold," added Mildred with a warm grin. "And we've still got a car seat in the back from driving our great-granddaughter around Washington."

I couldn't say no. I couldn't say anything, actually. My eyes filled with tears, and I didn't trust my voice, so I nodded gratefully, accepting her kindness.

"We sure do, littlebit," says Tom. "Black bears a'plenty. But no grizzlies, brown or polar."

"Urso's a grizzly," says Gia, holding up her beloved friend.

"Well," says Tom, "then I stand corrected. We got one grizzly on Prince of Wales Island now!"

Gia giggles with glee, telling Urso that he will need to make friends with the black bears since there are no other grizzlies around.

Mildred peeks around the seat, offering me a small smile. "She's a lovely child."

"Thanks," I say. "She's the love of my life."

"I feel the same about our daughter and granddaughters."

"And our great-granddaughter!" adds Tom. "She's Gia's age, and just as much of a pip."

I manage a small smile before turning my gaze to the window again.

"I don't mean to pry," continues Mildred, reaching for my kneecap and giving it a gentle pat, "but Craig is very small. Perhaps we know the person you're visiting? Tom said you're here to see family?"

Back on the ferry, when Tom asked if we were headed to Craig on vacation, I hadn't thought quickly enough to come up with a good lie and ended up saying we were surprising a cousin. In a town as small as Craig, however, it made sense that everyone knew everyone. And certainly, a transplant like Tony would stick out like a sore thumb.

"He's a, um—a cousin, from back home in New Jersey," I say, uncomfortable lying to these kind people. "Tony, um...?"

"Tony Silvestri? The handyman?" asks Tom, flicking a look at me in the rearview mirror. "We know Tony!"

"Tony's just charming!" gushes Mildred. "And so handsome! He built us the loveliest deck last year."

"We use it every night we can, don't we?" asks Tom, gazing at his wife with love.

"We surely do," agrees Mildred. She looks around the seat at me again, her eyes twinkling. "Well, isn't this just the nicest surprise?"

Nice? I think. *Ha. He probably hates my guts more than any other woman in the world.*

"Mmm," I hum, forcing a smile.

"I can't wait to see his face!" Mildred claps her hands together. "Since we know where he lives, we'll drop you off right at his doorstep to make sure you're taken care of."

"Great," I murmur, thinking "taken care of" can mean a lot of things.

Especially if you're from north Jersey.

***

Tony

It's a little after two on a Saturday afternoon and I'm in my front yard installing a new mailbox when Mildred and Tom Webster pull into my driveway.

More than good clients, they're a kindly older couple who've had me over to their house for dinner more than once. I like them. They've made Craig feel more like a home for me.

Squinting into the late afternoon sun, I think I can make out two people in the back of their SUV. Is their granddaughter visiting again? But weren't they just down in Seattle visiting her? Maybe she came back with them?

I take off my work gloves and shove them in my back pocket, walking up my driveway to the car. Before I get to Tom's window, Mildred jumps out of the passenger seat and yells:

"Surprise! Look who we found on the ferry!"

When you're on the run from the sort of people who

murdered my uncle in cold blood, the word "surprise" is the very last you want to hear. Instantly on guard, I freeze about ten feet away from the SUV, leaning down to take my gun from my ankle holster before remembering that I stopped carrying it around a few months ago. *Stupid! Foolish! You got too comfortable!* I straighten slowly, my heart rate tripling, and my hands start to shake.

As the door behind Tom opens slowly, my fight-or-flight response kicks in, and I race to find out who's tracked me down here. Maybe if I can get a sucker punch in first, I can disarm them before they can get a shot off at me.

But a second later, I find *I'm* the one disarmed.

A round, sweet face, framed with a riot of jet-black curls peeks around the side of the door, beaming at me with unabandoned delight. She jumps down from the car, raises her tiny arms over her head and stretches.

"Hi!" she says. "Are you Tony?"

I stare at her, baffled by her presence and identity, but not her accent. It's like music to my ears the way her little mouth pronounces "Are" like "Awhr." This kid is from Jersey. From home.

"Yeah," I say, unable to keep myself from grinning at her. "Who're you?"

"I'm Gia!" she says, giggling at me.

"Gia?" I say. "What's that short for? Gianna? Giovanna?"

"No!" she says, standing on one foot like a stork. "For *Gia*!"

"Well, Gia," I say, bending down to look into the back

of the car, hoping to find an adult that can give me more answers. "Where did youse come from, huh?"

There's no one back there. Whoever came here with Gia got out of the car at some point and has her back to the now-closed door. *Her*, because her long, dark hair riots past her shoulders and presses against the car window.

"From Newark," says Gia, "of course."

"Newark, huh?"

My skin prickles and my guard, which lowered upon meeting Gia, starts rising again.

I look over the top of the car, but I can't see anything. The person—*her mother?*—is so short, you can't see her over the top of the car.

"Who'd you come here with?" I ask the little sprite.

"My mamma, of course!"

"Tessa," says Tom, "come on over here and give your cousin a hug!"

Tessa? Cousin?

So, here's the thing… unless my family tree sprouted a branch I'm only learning about now, I don't *have* a cousin named Tessa.

Keeping my eyes trained on the front of the car, I finally see a woman come into view. No more than five-three, her face is as round as a soccer ball, and her body hasn't seen a treadmill in years. I scan back up, over her protruding belly and full breasts, to note that her skin is olive-toned, like mine. She's got eyelashes for days—sexy, long and black—like most Jersey girls, and her lips, plump and full, are painted fire engine red and shiny as chrome. The sight of them makes my cock twitch, which surprises me a little since fat chicks aren't my thing.

As she rounds the car, she keeps her eyes down, but just as she reaches Tom's window, she looks up at me, nailing me with deep brown eyes and a determined expression. And you know what? I have no idea who she is. None. I've never seen this woman in my entire life.

To add to the surrealness of the moment, out of nowhere, she throws herself against me, wrapping her arms around my waist. Although—or maybe *because*—I'm utterly stunned, my arms move of their own volition, pulling her body against mine and hugging her.

"You're thinking you don't know me from Adam," she mutters against my chest.

If I thought the kid's voice sounded welcome? Hers is like music. Probably rough-sounding to the rest of the world, it makes my eyes burn, it's so achingly familiar to me.

"Bingo," I say, my arms tightening around her.

"I'll explain, but for now, please play along?" she asks, her words soft and frantic. "Please?"

"Why should I?"

"'Cause I'm in trouble," she whispers. "And I had nowhere else to go."

Fuck. I can relate.

"Yeah. Fine," I say. "But you owe me… cuz."

"Yeah, yeah. I owe you."

I glance up at Tom, who's beaming at us, and give him a grin. "My cousin's here!"

"Surprised you, huh?" asks Tom.

"You have no idea," I say. "I haven't seen my lil' cuz, Tessa, since… since… well, I can't even remember how long it's been. Forever, maybe. Ha."

"Ha! Forever! Ha! A long time. A long, long time," agrees Tessa, finally loosening her arms from around my waist and taking a step away from me.

And me? I miss the feeling of her warm, round body against mine. I wouldn't have counted myself as one for hugs, really, but my Zia was a big hugger, and I guess I've been missing them.

"My turn!" squeals the kid, throwing her arms around my leg.

"And—ha ha!—she brought her kid to visit!" I say to Tom, not sure what to do about the tiny being now attached to my leg.

"Gia," says Tessa, "give the man—um, Cousin Tony, um, some space, baby."

Gia looks up at me, two dimples caving in her round cheeks, and I can't help but smile back. Damn, but this kid is cute.

"Gia!" says Tessa, using a "mom" voice. It's sharper, and something about it is vaguely familiar. Hmm. Maybe my mom used a tone like that with me when I was little? "Let's say goodbye to Mr. Tom and Miss Mildred, honey. I'm sure they want to be getting home now."

Gia releases my leg and races to the car to hug the Websters goodbye, and I dart a glance at Tessa, who's encouraging her to say "thank you" to Mildred. Meanwhile, Tom takes two hot pink and black rolling suitcases out of the trunk and places them in front of me.

"Nice girls," he says.

"Oh, yeah," I say. "Real nice."

"Tony!" says Mildred, making her way back to the passenger side of the car. "Why don't you and the ladies join us for dinner next Friday night?"

Tessa shoots me a glance, and I glare at her for a second before offering Mildred a smile. "Sounds terrific, Mildred. Thanks a bunch."

After exchanging hugs and goodbyes, Tom and Mildred pull out of my driveway, waving at the three of us until their car disappears down the street. I turn around, placing my hands on my hips and facing Tessa and Gia.

"So?" I say, staring down at them. "What the hell?"

Tessa raises her chin, her brown eyes wide and worried, though she's trying to look tough.

"I can explain."

"Fuck, yes, you will explain," I murmur.

Gia gasps. "You said a bad word."

"Get used to it," I tell her.

"I gotta do tinkles," she tells me.

"What's—"

"She's gotta pee," says Tessa, glancing at my house, then back at me.

Fuck, no. These two aren't coming into my house until I find out who they are and what the fuck they're doing here first.

"Mamma! It's cominggggg," Gia whines, grasping at her crotch and hopping from foot to foot.

Shit. Is the kid gonna take a piss in my driveway?

"Jesus! Get her inside," I say, gesturing impatiently to the front door.

Tessa places her hands on Gia's shoulders, leading her to the front door, while I grimace at the hot pink suitcases, which I now note are emblazoned with the word "Juicy" in rhinestones. Pulling the bags behind me, I note that Tessa's ass is, indeed, juicy—the roundest, juiciest ass I've seen in ages. While I don't usually go for a figure as filled out as hers, I suppose it helps that she's wearing tight black jeans that cup it close, and high heeled black shoes that force it up and out. Or maybe it's just that I haven't gotten some in a while. I shake my head in annoyance, dragging the suitcases behind me.

"Pull it open," I call to Tessa, who stands at the front door with a wiggly Gia. "John's the first door on the right."

They disappear inside and I pull their bags onto my front porch, and then into my foyer.

I park the bags next to the front door and close it behind me. Then I stand in the middle of the front hall, clasp my hands behind my back, and wait for the bathroom door to open.

The second they come out, we're having a chat.

And by "chat," I mean she's going to tell me who the fuck they are, and how the hell they landed on my doorstep today.

CHAPTER SEVEN

Tessa

He's pissed.

Fuck, he's pissed.

And he's hot.

So. Fucking. Hot.

He's pissed and he's hot, and surprisingly, he's being a good sport so far. He could've called my bluff in front of the Websters and told us to get lost, but he didn't. And that was kind of him. Super kind. Unexpectedly decent.

But I'm betting that kindness and decency would disappear in a New York second if he knew who I really was. Luckily, I introduced myself as Tessa to the Websters, and Tony didn't appear to make a connection between me and the mega-bitch, Theresa, who answered his ad and fileted him over the phone. Thank God.

"Mamma, I gotta do poopies, too."

"Yeah. That's fine," I say, checking out my reflection in the mirror. I look like a landmine. My shirt is stained from yesterday's dinner and so wrinkled, it's ridiculous. I reach into my purse and pull out some eyeliner and mascara, darkening my eyes and thanking Jesus for fresh extensions. "Go ahead and do your poopies, baby. Take your time."

Take your time because Mamma needs to figure out what story—

a.k.a., lie—to tell next.

I decide it's smartest to keep it simple and based on the fact that I used my cousin Rosemarie's picture to bait him, I'll just go ahead and pretend it was Rosemarie who contacted him, and that I learned about him through her: I remembered what she said about Craig being isolated, and decided to hide there.

"Theresa is Rosemarie, and Tessa is you," I whisper to my reflection as Gia flushes the toilet.

"I can't reach the sink," she says, so I lift her up and help her wash her hands before squatting down in front of her.

"Baby," I say. "Isn't Tony nice?"

"I like Tom and Mildred."

"Yeah, I know. They're like *Nonna e Nonno*, right?"

Gia nods. "I miss them."

"Yeah, me too, baby," I tell her, thinking I'm going to need to contact my parents in Italy before word gets around that I've disappeared from Newark. I don't want them to worry. "But Tony's super nice too. So, I need you to be a good girl, okay? A nice girl."

"Okay, Mamma."

"I'm gonna ask Tony if you can watch TV while he and I talk. And you're gonna sit there and watch TV like a good girl. No interrupting. No getting up. No asking for snacks, *capiche?*"

Gia nods solemnly, and I pull her close, burying my nose in her curls and telling her I love her to *la luna* and back.

"I love you to *la luna* and back too, Mamma."

I take her hand and open the door, not surprised to find Tony standing in the foyer, about five feet from us, hands on his hips, a pissed-off expression on his brutally handsome face. *Madonna*, but he wasn't lying. He is *beautiful*. Dark, wavy hair. Blue eyes. A muscular, tan body. It's *distracting* how gorgeous he is. And makes me feel fatter, frumpier and shabbier than I already felt. Smoothing my hands over my rumpled t-shirt, I muster a small smile.

"Um… could Gia watch TV while we talk?"

His eyes slide to my daughter, and I think his face softens a touch as he considers her. Finally, he shrugs, gesturing with annoyance to his living room. I usher Gia into the large, bright, open space and get her settled on the couch as Tony turns on the TV.

"Whaddashe like?"

"Um… a kid's show? Any kid's show?"

Tony flips through the channels until he comes across a cartoon, then places the remote on the glass coffee table in front of the couch.

He points at me. "You and me. Back deck. Now."

I follow him through sliding glass doors and onto a large deck with beautiful views of a harbor beyond. Sailboats bob in the afternoon sun and the water sparkles like it's dusted with diamonds.

"Oh!" I exclaim. "Look at this! It's… beautiful!"

"Yeah?" he says, closing the sliding door. "Yeah. It's nice."

"It's gorgeous."

"Don't try to butter me up," he says. "Take a seat. Explain this to me."

I turn around to find him sitting on the other side of a picnic table, and I plop down across from him, lacing my fingers together in front of me.

"It's like this," I begin. "Gia and I needed somewhere to go. Somewhere far away from Jersey…"

He stares at me, looking pissed.

"I'm waiting to hear how I factor into the equation."

"Well…" I gulp, cringing as I continue. "I have this cousin… um, Theresa?"

His eyes widen and he recoils, leaning back from the table as his lips thin into a small sneer.

"*Theresa.*" He whispers the name like a curse word.

Feeling nervous, I start speaking fast. "Um, so Theresa and me work together at my cousin's salon, and she was telling me about you a few weeks ago, and I remembered what she said about Craig, and how it was far away and in the middle of nowhere, and I—"

"*Theresa* is your… *cousin*?" he spits.

My heart rate triples from the dark look on his face. "Uh-huh."

"She's a bona fide, cold-blooded bitch, that one."

Slightly offended on her—I mean, *my*—behalf, I raise my chin. "You don't know her well enough to—"

"The fuck I don't."

"You don't know what she went through!" I bark back, thinking about Giancarlo, and all the other hot guys of the world who treat fat, plain girls like gum on their sole.

"I don't give a *steaming shit* what she went through," says Tony, using air quotes as he growls the words "went through." "She tore me a new asshole, and I didn't fucking deserve it."

It's my turn to wince. I hurt him. I really hurt him. And that feels terrible.

"I'm sorry for—um, sorry she did that."

He eyes me with utter disgust. "And you're her fucking cousin? Her family? Her blood?"

I nod. "Yeah. We work together."

"So, what the fuck are you doing here, *Theresa's cousin*?" he snarls, leaning away from the table, like he wants to put physical distance between us.

I lick my lips, lowering my shaking hands to my lap. He wouldn't hurt me, would he? Like, *physically* hurt me? I glance through the sliding doors, where my baby sits inside, on his couch, watching *Scooby Doo. Jesus, please don't let him hurt us.*

"Even though I knew you might hate her," I say, keeping my voice as level as possible, "coming here was safer than staying there."

"Well, then you must be in a *world* of shit," he says.

His eyes, a deep, dark blue, scan my face, softening just a little.

"I am," I murmur, nodding my head. "I'm in trouble."

"With who?"

I clench my teeth together, staring at him, trying to decide how much to share.

Here's the thing: the Italian-American world of northern New Jersey is small. The chance that he's heard of the Luciano crime family, and more specifically, of Santo or Vito D'Angelo, is high. The chance that someone he knows is allied with them? Probable. The chance that he knows them or works with them? Possible. Depending on Tony's loyalties, no matter what I say, I could be putting us in further danger.

"You don't want to tell me," he says. "You come to my doorstep—you bring this shitstorm to my doorstep—but you don't want to tell me? You've got balls, cuz."

"I've got fear," I correct him. "I'd do anything for…" I shoot another glance at the sliding glass doors. "I have to keep her safe."

His eyes narrow. "Someone's after… the kid?"

I nod. "Yeah."

"She doesn't belong to you?"

"She's *my* daughter!" I cry.

"Then…?"

"Someone else…" I pause, tears filling my exhausted eyes. "Someone else wants her. Wants to take her away from me."

"Does this someone else have a claim to her?"

"It's not her father," I say. At least about this, I can be honest. "Her father's dead."

Tony raises his chin, his eyes softening just a little more. He nods, taking a deep breath and letting it go. "*Mi dispiace.*"

"*Grazie,*" I whisper.

"How?" he asks.

"How… what?"

"How did he die?"

I blink my eyes furiously, then raise my shaking hand. I shape my fingers into a gun, point my index finger under my chin, then flick my thumb like a trigger.

He gasps. It's soft, but I hear it.

"I see," he says. He nods at me, and I feel the first little bit of relief since I arrived on Tony's doorstep. He's made a decision about us. He's going to let us stay. It's all going to be— "You gotta go. Now."

Wait. What?

I gulp, licking my lips as the rest of my body prickles with a sudden, unpleasant adrenaline boost. "Wh-what?"

He stands up from the picnic table, looking down at me, his expression severe. "You gotta go. I left Jersey to get away from shit like this. You… you gotta go."

"I have nowhere to go," I whisper, barely able to catch my breath.

"That's not my problem," he says, putting his hands on his hips. "Get your kid, get your bags, and go."

"Please—"

"Don't beg me. You've had balls up to now. Don't shame yourself," he says. "You gotta go."

Am I making this up based on how I'm feeling, or am I noticing fear—real, unadulterated fear—in his face, in his gestures, in his voice? I don't get up from where I'm sitting. If anything, I settle my fat ass onto the picnic bench a little more permanently.

"What are you scared of?" I ask him.

His eyes narrow. I've hit a nerve.

"Fuck you."

"You're scared," I say, pointing my finger at him. "You're so scared, you won't help a single mother and her little girl."

"Fuck you!" he shouts. "I don't owe you shit."

"True," I say, finally standing up. "And you know what? I don't want anything from you either. Better to stand tall on my own, than crouch next to a coward."

"I'm not a coward!" he says, crossing his muscular arms over his chest.

"All evidence to the contrary," I say, rounding the table. I stand in front of him, my eyes level with his beautiful mouth, then tilt my head back so we're eye-to-eye. "A big, strong man, but you're more scared than me." I shake my head, letting my face register all the disgust I feel. "Pathetic."

I pass him, stepping into his house, grabbing my daughter's hand and beelining for the foyer.

We walk out his front door without a second glance.

Good fucking riddance.

***

Tony

FUCK.

HER.

Who the *fuck* does she think she is?

I stride back into my house, slamming my front door before leaning against it, my muscles bunched up into knots, my heart pumping with equal parts of fear and shame.

"Fuck you!" I bellow, the sound of my fury bouncing off the marble floor of my empty foyer. "Fuck you… and…

and fuck your cute kid, too! Fuck both of youse!"

Pushing away from the door, I go into my living room and turn off the TV, scrubbing my hands through my hair and falling back onto my couch.

She triggered me. She triggered me by talking about her bitch cousin, and then by making that—that *obscene* gesture with her fingers to her chin. The sound of a gunshot roars in my head and a flashback of my uncle's lifeless head thudding onto his desk makes me shiver.

Fuck, no, I'm not inviting that madness back into my life. *Forget it.*

But her face.

Christ. The disgust on her face.

Better to stand tall on my own, than crouch next to a coward.

The memory of her words makes me wince, makes my heart hurt, makes me ball up my fists with fury and impotence. How dare she? How fucking *dare* she call me a coward?

Was she there? Did she see what I saw? Did she watch her uncle be murdered?

No. No. And no.

She has no right to judge me.

"Fucking bitch!" I scream, throwing the remote control across the room. It lands in my fireplace, breaking against the brick lining, batteries and splinters of black plastic shattered in the ash.

Seeds of shame sprout from the pit of my stomach into climbing vines that weave and rise until they fill my throat like a giant lump of weeds that I can't swallow over.

You are a coward.

For shame.

The two of them are walking up the road from my house with their hot pink suitcases and unsuitable footwear, their perilous situation unknown to every soul in town but me. They have nowhere to go, and everything to lose if they don't stay hidden.

And me? I know better than anyone how to hide. And not only that, but I also have a plan for if I'm found. I think of my small arsenal of weapons in the basement: two Glocks, a Savage 30-06 with a Bushnell scope, a Sig Sauer with 350 rounds, a papoose for wearing it all at once, and a sub-compact 9mm pistol that's going back on my ankle today.

When I moved here, I acquired what I needed to survive. Can she say the same? Does she have appropriate protection hidden somewhere in those ridiculous suitcases?

Fuck. Fuck, fuck, fuck.

The last thing I need is a single mom and her kid complicating my simple life, but the thought of them being found and threatened bugs me. It bugs me a lot, actually.

No, Tessa's not my dream girl, and yes, her cousin is a fucking *sciacquata*, but taken on her own, Tessa didn't seem so bad to me. She was brave, but desperate. And fuck, but I remember how that felt.

"Fuck!" I yell, getting up from the couch. I grab my truck keys from the kitchen counter and head out a side door into my garage.

They can't have gotten very far.

CHAPTER EIGHT

Tessa

My feet hurt.

My muscles are screaming.

My head aches with every step.

This road is rough and gravelly, and I'm pulling two suitcases behind me, one of which is a makeshift stroller for Gia, who's perched on top, sitting with her back against the raised handle, and adding thirty-five pounds to what I'm pulling.

I have no idea where we're going, but I hope I'm headed toward a town because I need a bed. When I get one, I'm falling into it, closing my eyes and sleeping until tomorrow.

"Car's coming, Mamma."

"They can fucking pass us."

"You said a bad word," she informs me.

"Yeah, yeah," I huff. "Mamma's pulling everything we got. Including you. She's entitled to a few bad words."

"Mamma, I think he's slowing down."

"Who?"

"Tony."

"*Il vigliacco*," I murmur. *The coward.*

I get it that the double whammy of being "Theresa's" cousin and on the run was enough to make him think twice about letting us stay, but kicking us out into the street? I didn't expect that. Once he agreed to play along, I thought I could convince him to let us stay.

My mistake. Tony's just another beautiful, empty suit. All flash. No substance. Just like Giancarlo, who never offered me, or his daughter, anything real, like his name or his protection.

As the truck rolls to a stop about twenty feet in front of us, I pause in my progress, tilting the suitcases upright and putting my hands on my hips.

What does he want now?

He exits the truck, running a hand through his hair as he approaches us with his head down, his eyes tracking the ground. And damn it, but when he raises his head, I wish the sight of those dark blue eyes didn't affect me, but they do. I've always been weak for a beautiful man. Fuck him for being so gorgeous.

"Get in the truck," he barks, stopping about six feet away from me, an annoyed expression on his face.

"No, thank you."

"Like you got so many better offers? Don't be dumb. Get in the truck."

"Fuck you."

"Mamma!" cries Gia, slapping my butt.

"Don't be fresh!" I tell her, then turn my attention back to Tony. "We'll find a hotel."

"That way?" he asks. "Okay. But one problem: the only

business down this road is the Prince of Wales Shooting Club, and last I checked, they're not a hotel." He holds up his hands. "But you do you."

Fuck me.

"We'll go the other way."

"You could," he says, "But it's about six miles to town." He glances down at my shoes. "So, good luck with that."

Six fucking miles? Are you shitting me here?

I take a deep breath, and then—to my shock and shame—a sob rips from my throat, and my eyes, which were dry as bone a moment ago, flood with tears. Suddenly, I'm treating Tony to the most pitiful, fucking blubber fest you can imagine.

I stand there on the side of the street with no plan and nowhere to go… and I cry.

I cry for Giancarlo, who's dead, and for Gia, who will never know her father.

I cry that my parents are so far away when I need them so badly, and my cousins couldn't be bothered to help me look after my daughter.

I cry because I've done this man wrong twice now—once on the phone, calling him a shallow asshole, and once in his own house, calling him a coward.

I cry because my feet are blistered and bleeding, and my body's exhausted.

I cry because I don't know how to keep my daughter safe.

I cry because I don't think I'll ever feel safe again.

I cry until snot's hanging from my nose and my tears have soaked my shirt, and—*Lord help me*—I still have more to cry.

I have no idea when Tony puts his arms around me and pulls me roughly against his chest, but I don't have the strength to push him away, so I lean against him, *into him*, closing my eyes and weeping. I feel Gia latch on to my leg, her little voice repeating, "It's okay, Mamma. It's going to be okay," like I do when she's sad or hurt. We're a single organism of three separate, displaced beings, clustered together on the side of the road, in the middle of nowhere, Alaska.

Finally, when the well is dry, I take a deep, shuddering breath and I open my burning eyes. The first thing I see is that my boogers and tears have soaked Tony's shirt too, and I mumble an apology through sniffles and hiccups.

"S-Sorry," I say. "I don't… I don't know what just ha-happened."

"It's okay," he says, his voice surprisingly gentle.

"See, Mamma?" says Gia, her voice tinged with worry as she looks up at my tear-stained face. "It's okay. It's going to be okay."

I swipe at my eyes with the backs of my hands and squat down at eye level with her.

"Oh, baby. I'm okay. Sometimes mammas cry, too."

"I know," she says, her own eyes watering, her lower lip quivering. "But it's s-scary."

"Don't be scared." I force a smile as I pull her into my arms. "I'm okay now, baby. I promise I'm okay."

She clings to me like a baby monkey, so I hold her close as I straighten up. My eyes find Tony's looking down at us, his expression troubled, but gentler than before.

"Will you get in the fucking truck now?" he asks me. I nod at him, reaching around for our suitcases, but he stops me. "I'll get 'em. You two get in."

I hear the suitcases hit the bed of the truck as I open the passenger door and sit down in the front seat with Gia straddling my lap. A moment later, Tony swings his body into the truck and sits down beside us.

"You're a piece of work, you know that?"

Uncertain of how to respond, I shrug. "Not usually."

This is the truth—I prefer to fly below the radar.

"I highly doubt that," he mutters, putting the truck into drive and making a wide U-turn in the middle of the empty street.

The truck makes quick work of retreading our steps, and a few seconds later we're back in Tony's driveway, his log cabin-style house standing sturdy and tall before us. He cuts the engine and turns to me.

"My basement's finished. I got a bar and a john down there, and a big couch. You know, for watching games and stuff. You can stay there."

For how long?

The words sit on the tip of my tongue, but I don't dare say them, already having tested his patience more than once today.

"I'll look for a job tomorrow," I tell him. "As soon as I find one, I'll get us set up somewhere else."

"Yeah, well," he says, looking doubtful, "there's only one salon in town and I don't know if they're hiring."

"I can do other things," I say, thinking I'll do whatever it takes: work a register, wait tables, clean houses. My father always insisted that there was always a job someone else didn't want if you were willing to work. "I'll find something."

"The library's looking for someone," he says. "But it's only part-time."

"Part-time's okay. Gotta start" —I can't hold back a yawn— "somewhere."

"You're tired."

"You have no idea," I tell him, unsurprised to note that Gia's fallen asleep in my lap, her small head using my breasts as a pillow. "We left Newark at four yesterday."

"And you haven't slept since?"

I shake my head. "Not a wink."

He grimaces, then nods. "We need some ground rules if you're going to stay here for a few nights, but we can talk tomorrow. Let's get youse settled first."

I carry a sleeping Gia inside, following Tony to a door off the kitchen, and down carpeted stairs into a beautiful basement. There's a large, cream-colored leather sectional, big enough for Gia and I to share, a massive TV, a small bar area with a fridge and microwave, and a tiny bathroom with a toilet and sink. Sliding doors lead outside onto a patio under the deck.

Something deep inside of me is soothed by the sweeping views of the harbor, and I stand at the window, willing myself not to cry.

"This is beautiful," I murmur, still cradling my sleeping daughter in my arms. "Thank you for letting us stay."

"You'll have to shower upstairs," he says, parking our suitcases against a wall. "If you need to use the kitchen, that's fine, too."

I place Gia on the sectional, covering her with a bright green Jets blanket.

"There's more blankets under the TV," he says, gesturing to a cabinet. Then he points at a door beside the bathroom door. "Don't go in there. Don't let the kid near it."

"What's in there?" I ask, scanning his face for clues.

"We got bears here," he says. "Gray wolves, too."

"Guns," I murmur, holding his eyes.

He nods. "But it's locked up. Just… leave it alone."

"Yeah," I say. "Okay."

He raises his hands. "Anything else?"

I shake my head. "Thanks, again."

"Yeah," he says, looking unhappy. "We'll talk tomorrow, yeah?"

"Yeah," I say, feeling faint from weariness.

As his footsteps fade up the stairs, I have just enough energy to toe off my shoes, pull a second Jets blanket from the cabinet under the TV, lie down head-to-head with my daughter, and draw the green fleece over my exhausted body.

***

Tony

It's not like Saturday nights are hopping in downtown Craig, but I've been known to hit the Hill Bar or The Craig Inn from time to time, especially if Jim joins me.

Because Monday is Labor Day, the unofficial end of summer, the Hill sets up tables outside and The Craig Inn flies in a band from Seattle. It's a street party in town tonight, and I'm not missing it on account of my surprise houseguests.

After finishing my mailbox installation, showering my stanky ass, and slipping into clean jeans and a crisp white t-shirt, I tiptoe down to my basement to check on the girls. It's after eight, but it won't be dark until ten o'clock, so I lower the blackout shades over the sliding glass doors, blocking out the late-day sun that would have hit Tessa's eyes in the next hour or so.

I put a bag of potato chips and two bottles of water on the ottoman in case they wake up, moving quietly as they snore softly.

The kid is tiny, all curled up in a ball under her blanket, her black curls rioting over the cream leather of my couch. She's so fucking little. So vulnerable. I haven't been around a child in so long, I'd forgotten how small they were.

Older than my three younger cousins back in Bayonne, I'd grown up babysitting for Lena, Carla, and Bella whenever my Zia Marina and Uncle Gino wanted a night out. I didn't relish changing diapers or wiping snotty noses, but I knew my place in my aunt and uncle's household. As the only child of my Zia Marina's dead brother, Mario, I was deeply loved and well cared for by my aunt and uncle, but being helpful to them ensured the goodwill that made living with them that much more comfortable. Over the years, they came to regard me as the son they never had, with my uncle even grooming me to take over his share of the family business someday.

I take a deep breath, shutting the door on painful memories and turning my attention to Tessa. Sleeping on her back with one arm thrown over her head, the blanket had slipped down to reveal the swells of her breasts under a clingy t-shirt.

You're a big girl.

You've got a fat ass, thick limbs, wide hips, and a double chin.

And fat isn't hot. Right?

I narrow my eyes, pulling the blanket up to her chin, careful not to graze her breasts with the backs of my fingers. Scrubbing my hand over the five o'clock shadow on my chin, I tilt my head to the side and frown.

Usually right.

The truth is that I can't deny, in her own big-girl way, Tessa's got something going on. An *attractive* thing. A *sexy* thing.

Her hair is long, black and glossy, and her lips are plump. She obviously cares about how she looks—wearing those uncomfortable heels on a cross-country trip—and damn it, but she's a good mother. She puts her daughter's safety above everything else. Her kid was threatened by someone, so she packed up and split. Flown, ferried and driven to Craig, Alaska, because she'd heard about it once, and it sounded like the ends of the earth. Like a good place to hide.

I wonder if my own mother once loved me as fiercely as Tessa loves Gia. I was only six when she and my father passed away, so my memories of her are lean. I remember the way she smelled—like VO5 hairspray, cold cuts and my father's cigarette smoke—and that she always wore gold bracelets on her wrist that clinked together when she moved her arms. Her laugh was tinkly, like wind chimes, and her hugs were warm and full-bodied.

Would she have hidden with me in Craig, Alaska, at the home of a virtual stranger, if it meant keeping me safe?

Glancing at my gun closet, I cross the room softly, taking a keyring out of my pocket. As quickly and quietly as possible, I unlock the door, unlock the safe, and remove my 9mm, checking the magazine before securing it in my ankle holster.

Then, I lock up the safe and closet and tiptoe back upstairs.

***

"So!" says Jim once we've got two full pints of beer and an outdoor picnic table at which to drink them. "I was talking to Mildred Webster, who told me we've got some newcomers in town! I didn't know your cousin was coming to visit!"

"Neither did I," I tell him. "She, uh, surprised me."

"Is she hot?"

I frown at him. "She's my cousin."

"So what? Is she good-looking or not?"

"She's big, but she's not… ugly."

"Wow. Don't sing her praises too loud, now. I wouldn't

want you to hurt yourself."

"She's got a kid."

Jim nods like this doesn't bother him at all. "Cool. How old?"

"Little."

"A baby?"

"No. She talks… and tinkles."

Jim, whose sister has three little kids, chuckles. "Four? Five?"

"Somewhere around there."

"When can I meet her?"

"The kid? She's a little young for you."

"Don't be disgusting. The mom."

I don't want you to meet her.

The thought zips through my head at the speed of light but leaves a bad taste in my mouth. I don't own Tessa. I barely know her. She could do a lot worse than Big Jim Kerrigan.

I shrug. "Whenever you want. She's applying for the job at the library. Stop by next week and pretend you know how to read."

"I'll have you know that I enjoy reading."

"Cereal boxes?"

"Shut-uppa-you-mouth," says Jim, pursing his fingers together and shaking them at me.

I shake my head at his terrible impression of an Italian-American accent. "Amateur."

"Who's an amateur and at what?"

Jim and I look up at the same time to see Rachel

Morehouse standing beside our table, a brown sack of groceries balanced on her left hip. My eyes slide to Jim's face, watching—with fascination—the instant transformation there, from relaxed to alert, from easy-going to laser-focused.

"Hey, Rachel," he says, his already-ruddy cheeks pinkening.

"Hi, Jim," she says, giving him a sweet smile before turning to me. "Hi, Tony."

"How *you* doin'?" I ask, mimicking Joey Tribbiani from *Friends*.

She giggles. "You do that better than anyone."

"Hey! Bada bing, bada boom! I'm a Jersey boy!"

Jim finally looks away from Rachel, shaking his head at me. "You're a ham, is what you are."

I shrug, taking a long sip of beer as the band starts playing "Brown-Eyed Girl."

"Rachel," asks Jim, "you want a beer? I could get you one."

She shakes her head. "No, thank you, Jim. I have to get these groceries home. I have ice cream for my dad."

"How's he doing?" asks Jim.

She bites her lower lip and I watch Jim's eyes widen. *Man, he really likes her. How the fuck did I miss this before?*

"He's okay, I guess. His spirits are low."

What else is new? Nasty sonofabitch.

"That's too bad," says Jim. "Want me to come over sometime? Watch a game with him? Hawks are playing the Colts next Sunday."

"Oh, Jim! How kind! He'd love it." Rachel's face brightens with the wattage of her smile. "What time does the game start? I'll make snacks for you two!" She slides her eyes over to me, and though I'm hoping I don't see interest in them, I'm pretty sure I do. *Shit.* She licks her lips. "Tony, you're welcome too."

"Nah," I say. "My team's the Jets."

And my best friend is Jim.

"But you could still come," she presses.

Kill this, I think. *Kill it now, for Jim's sake.*

"No, thanks," I say. "Your dad's a lot."

Her smile disappears and hurt fills her eyes. "A… *lot?*"

"Yeah," I say, feeling bad for whatever pain I'm causing her, but eager to put Jim's interests first. "I can think of better ways to spend an afternoon than hanging out with your dad."

"Bro!" exclaims Jim, looking at me in surprise. "Don't be an asshole."

"No," says Rachel, lifting her chin. "That's fine, Jim. Go ahead and be an asshole, Tony. True colors don't lie."

"I'll still be there, Rachel," says Jim. "One o'clock kickoff. Does one work for you?"

"Sure." All the enthusiasm for the plan has drained from her pretty face, making her look tired. "I'll see you then."

As she turns and walks away, Jim bellows, "Looking forward to it already!" before turning to me with a murderous expression in his eyes. "What the *fuck*, Tony?"

I can't very well tell him that I think Rachel is—*was?*—

still attracted to me, so I shrug. "Sorry, man. I was just being honest. Her dad's not exactly a bucket of laughs."

"She takes care of him, you monumental douchebag!"

"Yeah, I know," I say. "You should be thanking me. You don't want me there. Now you get Rachel all to yourself, right?"

He considers this for a second. "I mean, yeah… I guess. But you didn't have to be such an asshole to her."

Planting his elbows on the table, he ignores me as he waves a few friends over to our table.

Jim's wrong, though.

Sometimes, being an asshole is the kindest weapon in a man's arsenal.

CHAPTER NINE

Tessa

When I wake up, I have no idea where I am.

But my neck hurts… and my cheek is stuck to plastic.

No, not plastic. Leather. Leather?

Why am I sleeping on leather? Where the fuck am I?

My eyes flutter open, and it's dark except for the outline of bright white light in a rectangle in front of me.

I peel my cheek off the sectional and sit up, groaning at the stiffness of my neck and finally remembering that I'm in Alaska. I reach around for my phone before remembering that I purposely left it at my apartment in Newark on Friday night. I didn't want the D'Angelos to be able to trace my whereabouts.

Looking to my left, I expect to see Gia and panic that her blanket is balled up in the corner of the sectional.

"Gia?" I call, standing up.

I rush over to the bathroom on creaky knees and open the door, but it's empty.

Running up the basement stairs in bare feet, I burst into the first floor of Tony's house.

"Gia!" I scream.

"Over here, Mamma!" she calls from the other side of the door.

I slam it shut, relief making my shoulders slump as I find her perched on a high stool at the kitchen counter. In front of her is a plate of pancakes. Across from her, flipping pancakes on a small, freestanding griddle, is Tony Silvestri, wearing a pair of jogging shorts and a grin.

"Morning," he says.

"G-Good morning," I say, my mouth watering. *At the pancakes? The sight of his bare chest?* It's a draw.

"Coffee?" he asks.

"*Madonna*, yes."

He chuckles, turning around to fill a coffee cup and giving me a perfect view of his muscular back, which tapers into the waistband of his navy-blue sports shorts. *Mamma mia.*

When he turns around, I'm not quick enough lifting my glance, and he catches me ogling.

"Like what you see?" he asks, laughing at me.

I snap my neck up, reaching for the coffee cup and taking a sip of the scalding brew. I cough in surprise, gasping for breaths of cool air.

"Careful, now," he says, his grin widening at my misfortune.

"You okay, Mamma?" asks Gia between bites of pancake.

"Hot, hot, hot!"

"Why, thank you," says Tony, his eyes twinkling.

"Not you! The coffee!"

"Whatever you say," he tells me, placing two pancakes on a plate and sliding it across the empty counter. "Hungry?"

"Starving," I say.

"I mean, for food," he clarifies, still having a terrific time at my expense.

I roll my eyes at him, taking the fork he offers me, and cutting off a corner of fluffy pancake. "Mmmm. Oh, my God. Incredible."

"Yeah," he says, equal parts cocky and teasing. "That's what they tell me."

"The p-pancake!" I sputter.

He chuckles again, flipping two more cakes onto a waiting plate and turning off the griddle. I watch as he slathers them with butter, then covers them in syrup.

"Tony's taking me to the beach today," announces Gia, taking a gulp of juice before attacking her second pancake. "But it's different from Wildwood, Mamma. I can't swim. It's too cold."

"And there are whales in the harbor," Tony reminds her.

"Yep," she says. "Whales."

I'm not sure how I feel about Tony and Gia making plans together, but I need to stop by the library today for a job application so maybe it's not such a bad idea for her to be occupied.

"Is the beach in the same direction as the library?" I ask.

"Nope." Tony shakes his head. "But the library's not open on Sundays."

"Oh."

"You'll have to wait until tomorrow."

"Huh," I say, taking a sip of my cooling coffee. "Well, I should get some groceries. And I'd like to call my parents."

He looks up at me, his eyes darkening. "Bad idea."

"What? Why?"

"You have a lot to learn."

He's right, of course.

"But I need to let them know we're okay," I insist.

"It's better to disappear."

"I can't do that to them."

"Then email them from my computer," he says, his face serious. "I use a Swiss encryption service called ProtonMail. It'll be a lot tougher to track you down."

"Is that really necessary?"

"Um… yeah. It's necessary."

"Why?"

He puts down his fork and plants his hands on the kitchen counter. "You can track a call from any phone; even a pay phone. So, calls to or from your parents without a scrambler are off-limits. It's too risky. And if you sent an email from here, from your regular account, it would have a time stamp. Out of the twenty-four time zones in the world, you'd be narrowing your location to one."

I stare at him, dumbstruck. I'd never even thought of that.

"Whatever you do, keep it short," he continues. "No indication of where you are or what you're doing. 'Hi, Mom and Dad. I'm safe. I'll be in touch. Tessa.'"

"And Gia!" says my daughter.

"And Gia," says Tony, his face relaxing a touch as he grins at her.

"If that's all I can say, what's the point of writing at all?" I ask, a lump filling my throat as I imagine how frightened my parents will be when they receive my cold, uninformative email.

But I have to admit that Tony's advice is sound and smart.

When I didn't show up to the wake, did Santo send someone to my apartment? He won't find much there. I left my phone in Newark and most of my wallet in the garbage can of an airport bathroom. Has he reached out to my parents? To my aunt, uncle, and cousins? He wouldn't hurt them in an effort to get information about me, would he? How far will he go to discover Gia's whereabouts?

As if reading my mind, Tony asks, "You didn't bring your cell phone, did you?"

"I'm not stupid," I murmur.

"What ID did you show at the airport?"

I cringe. *Maybe I am stupid.*

"My passport."

He nods. "You had to show them something to get through security, and you didn't have enough time to get decent forgeries. How did you get here?"

"What do you mean? By plane."

"No. I mean, what route did you take?"

"Jersey to Seattle. Seattle to—"

"Did you go back through security at Seattle? Show

your ID again?"

I have to think for a second. "No. I'm pretty sure we didn't."

"But you got on a different plane?"

I nod. "Yes."

"Okay. That's good. You could've gone anywhere in the U.S.," he says. "I trust a guy in Florida. You can send a quick email to your parents today over ProtonMail, but then we'll set up a new email address for you and have him send another message from Boca next week. Keep them guessing."

"Them?"

"Whoever you're running from."

My head is starting to pound.

"Mamma, can Urso and I go watch TV?"

"If it's okay with Tony," I say, looking up at him.

"Sure," he says, rounding the kitchen counter and following Gia to the living room where he turns the Cartoon channel on for her.

I gather our breakfast plates and coffee cups, taking them to his sink and turning on the hot water.

For the first time since we started talking this morning, I wonder: How does Tony know so much about this? About escaping. About hiding. About not being found.

I squeeze soap into the water and sponge off the plates, thinking about our last few conversations: *I left Jersey to get away from shit like this… Don't go in there. Don't let the kid near it… I use a Swiss encryption service called ProtonMail… I trust a guy in Florida.*

My hands still, dropping a clean plate back into the sudsy water.

Holy shit.

Tony's on the run, too.

***

Tony

After I set up the kid with cartoons, I head upstairs to take a shower and change. It's in the high fifties now, but it'll hit sixty-eight later, with bright, strong sun. As I exit my bathroom with a towel around my waist, I decide that shorts and a t-shirt would be ideal for a day at the beach.

"You're hiding here."

"Fuck!" I exclaim, freezing in the bathroom doorway, shocked to find Tessa sitting on the edge of my bed. Downstairs I can hear Gia's cartoons. "What the fuck?"

"I don't know why I didn't realize it yesterday. Because I was so tired, I guess. You're hiding here. You're on the run, just like me."

I eye her for a second, taking a deep breath before stepping into the room.

"So what?"

"So, you could've told me!" she says.

"Honestly, cuz?" I say, nailing her with an "eat shit" look. "It's none of your fucking business. You came here uninvited, remember?"

"Yeah, I remember," she says. "But—"

"No buts," I tell her, crossing the room and standing in front of my dresser. "Get outta my room. I gotta change."

"We need to talk," she says. "What happened to you?"

I whirl around. "What happened to *you*?"

"I told you," she says, her gaze slipping briefly to my bare chest before trailing back up to my face. Her cheeks are pink when she meets my eyes again. "Someone wants to take Gia away from me."

"Who?" I ask, wondering about those pink cheeks. She likes what she sees, huh? What surprises me, however, is how much I like her looking at me. She's sitting on my bed in aqua-colored silky shorts and a matching tank top, and I like that too.

"Her paternal grandfather."

This information makes me stop ogling her back and get serious. "Who's he?"

She bites her bottom lip.

"Quit that," I snap.

"Huh?"

"It's distracting," I mutter. "Who's Gia's grandfather?"

Her eyes widened when I barked at her about her lip, but now she blinks at me, as though clearing her head. "I'm scared to tell you."

"Baby, I hate to break it to you, but you're in the bedroom of a guy you met yesterday. You've figured out you're both on the run from something, and your kid needs protection. At this point, you've got nothing to lose by coming clean with me."

Her voice is slow and cautious when she speaks. "You're Italian and you're from… Bayonne, right?"

I nod at her.

"You've heard of the Luciano crime family?"

A chill runs down my spine as I nod again.

She gulps, mustering her courage to continue. "There's a family in Newark. They're part of the Luciano organization. Their name is, um… they're the, um…" Her eyes widen and her chest rises and falls dramatically with every breath she takes.

"Is Gia…" *Fuck, fuck, fuck.* "Is Gia a… D'Angelo?"

Her jaw tightens and for a second, I hope—*for the love of Christ, I hope*—she doesn't nod. But my hopes are dashed when she jerks her head up and down.

"Her biological dad was Giancarlo D'Angelo," she murmurs.

A shiver races down my spine, and my eyes shutter closed as I flashback to the last time I saw Gia's dad.

Do it, Giancarlo. He's a fucking rat bastard. Do it.

But Bayonne's not our territory—

Now it will be! Fucking pop him, son, or I will.

The sound of gunfire ricochets in my head and I turn away from Tessa, reaching blindly for the top of my bureau and steadying myself by leaning against it.

When I open my eyes, the silence in my bedroom is so deathly, I wonder if she's gone back downstairs, but when I turn around, she's still sitting on the edge of my bed, tears in her eyes, worrying her hands in her lap.

"Tony?" she squeaks.

My gut instinct is to tell her to get out of my room, out of my house, out of my life, like I did yesterday, but I can't. Something inside of me has changed since then, and I can't send her and Gia out into the world with no protection. Especially now.

"You know them?" she asks. "The D'Angelos?"

Better than I'd like.

I take a deep breath and nod at her, staring at her watery eyes and wondering what the fuck I'm about to get myself into.

"Yeah, I know them." Suddenly, something occurs to me. "Wait a second. Giancarlo is Gia's dad?"

"Biological, yeah."

"But you said her dad was dead."

"Yeah." She nods, a tear snaking down her cheek. "He was found in the Pines last week."

The Pine Barrens. Fuck. He got popped.

While this doesn't entirely surprise me—the D'Angelos had a nasty habit of trying to steal territory from other families—I had thought of them as mostly impregnable. Who, I wonder, my mind spinning wildly, had the balls to put out a hit on Giancarlo D'Angelo?

"Shit."

"Yeah."

"So Santo wants Gia."

She nods. "I should never have taken her to the funeral. It was—it was the stupidest mistake of my life, but I thought… I don't know… I guess I thought she had a right to go to her father's funeral."

"What does his funeral have to do with anything?" I ask.

"Oh. That's where Santo met her," she says, then adds

softly, "for the first time."

My head spins. Again.

How was that possible? How did Giancarlo and Tessa keep Gia a secret from the D'Angelos?

I'm still leaning against my bureau in a towel. "I gotta change. You wanna turn around?"

She pivots slightly on the bed, giving me her back. I grab underwear, a t-shirt, and some gray mesh shorts from my dresser, letting the towel fall to the floor and dressing quickly.

"Explain to me how Santo didn't know about her."

"I wasn't… I mean… I was Giancarlo's… um…"

I think about Tessa—about her huge tits, round tummy and fat ass—and answer my own question. He'd never be seen in public with her. She was his comfort fuck, not his girlfriend.

"You were his side piece."

"Mm-hm," she whispers.

"He didn't acknowledge you."

"Or her," she says, her voice laced with shame.

"*Brutto figlio di puttana bastardo,*" I mutter, feeling furious on behalf of Tessa and Gia.

So, Tessa may not be a supermodel, but fuck, she has more balls than most men I knew, and she isn't ugly, just chunky. And the kid? Cutest kid I ever saw. I would've been proud to claim her if I was him. But, then again, I'd never admired Giancarlo D'Angelo for his brains. He was a pompous asshole who coasted along on his good looks, his family's money, and their notoriety. He was a shallow, self-absorbed—

You're shallow, Tony. You're a shallow person. You're rich and good-looking and you feel like any girl should be grateful to land you, like you're some giant fucking prize… I've known guys like you all my life… You're not a good person, Tony…

Out of nowhere, snippets of the conversation I had with Tessa's cousin, Theresa, come rushing back to me, and her words make more sense now placed in the context of how Tessa was treated by Giancarlo. If Theresa was close to Tessa, she knew how Giancarlo had treated her, and she was pissed at men—*all men, me included*—for the way her cousin had been treated.

Do better next time. With the next girl.

I turn around, fully dressed, and look at Tessa, letting my eyes rest on her.

Her dark hair is up in a messy bun and her tank top clings to the rolls on her back. But for the first time, I don't really see her body. Or I do, but I don't evaluate it. I don't judge it. I don't label it. I don't call it "fat" in my mind, or think she'd be hotter if she lost weight, or anything else. It just is what it is.

She's just Tessa. A girl from Jersey. Theresa's cousin. Gia's mom.

Brave. Smart. Desperate.

And terrifyingly naïve about the choices she's made.

Inside of me, I feel my own protective instincts fire up, and suddenly I'm determined to be her safe harbor in a D'Angelo shitstorm. It's the least I can do after what happened to my uncle Gino. I mean, I couldn't save him…

but maybe I can save her.

Do better next time.

"You decent?" she asks.

"Debatable," I joke.

She looks at me over her shoulder, offering me a very small, very uncertain smile.

"Nah," she says softly, her words holding a double meaning that I cherish; that I want to live up to. "You're decent, Tony."

"Am I?" I ask her, thinking of how I hid behind the heavy drapes in my uncle's office when Santo and Giancarlo came to the house that dark and terrible night.

My uncle told me to hide, and I followed his orders in that request, as in everything else.

Don't come out, Antonio. No matter what. Don't come out.

I didn't. I didn't show myself, even when the argument turned from tense conversation to angry shouting. Even when I realized what Santo and Giancarlo intended. Even when Giancarlo lined up the pistol at my uncle's temple. Even when Uncle Gino's eyes caught mine briefly and issued a silent farewell.

I stayed hidden.

I let him die at the D'Angelo's hands.

I was a coward. A big fucking *vigliacco.*

Here it is, I think to myself, locking my eyes with hers. *A chance to do better.*

"You *are,*" she says with a rueful chuckle. "You've *got* to be… or I'm dead."

"That's not going to happen," I tell her firmly, putting

my hands on my hips as my resolve to help her strengthens. I've been hidden here for years now. I know how to do this. I can teach her how to hide, too. "You're not going to die. And Gia's not going back to them. I'm going to protect you. Both of you."

She shudders, her face contorting with a mixture of relief and gratitude. Her shoulders shake as she lowers her head, so I can't see her tears, but I can hear them.

I sit down on the edge of the bed and put my arm around her shoulders, pulling her close, and letting her rest her head against my chest.

"We'll figure this out together," I promise her, offering whatever safety I can. "No one's going to hurt you."

Dio mio, I pray, *let it be so.*

CHAPTER TEN

Tessa

The following morning, I call to arrange an interview at the Craig Free Library. I'm told to come in at ten o'clock, when the library opens, and to my surprise, I'm offered the position on the spot.

"We're really in desperate straits here," says Mrs. Finneman, the gray-haired, sharp-eyed library director, gesturing to a messy stack of books in the nearby RETURNS bin. "As long as you can start tomorrow, the job's yours."

"Yes!" I smile with delight. "I can be here tomorrow. Of course. Thank you! Yes!"

"Hours are ten to four, four days a week, Tuesday thru Friday. No benefits."

"That's fine," I tell her, grateful for a job—*any* job.

"We'll do a bit of training," she tells me, "but most of what you'll learn will be on-the-job. Answering the phones, checking books in and out, setting up the community room for scheduled events, meeting the school bus for after-school homework help, and monitoring the computers. Folks are only allowed to use them for an hour at a time, and we need to be firm."

"I can be firm," I assure her.

"You said you have a daughter?"

"Yes. Gia. She's four."

"She can't come to work with you, I'm afraid. We tried that once with a previous employee and it was too distracting. Do you have childcare set up?"

"I thought I might ask Mildred and Tom Webster if they could look after her."

"The Websters are good folks," says Mrs. Finneman, "but they're getting on in years. Why don't you check out the Craig Child Care Center? It's located just up the street. They take kids from ages three up to twelve."

"I will! I'll stop by today."

"Tell them Thelma Finneman sent you over and you've got the assistant job at the library. They'll fit Gia in."

"Thank you," I say, touched by her no-nonsense kindness.

"Now," she says, patting my application. "I'll just need to xerox your ID and social security card for tax purposes."

I stare at her for a second, feeling conflicted. I have my passport with me, and I know my social security number by heart, but what would Tony say? I can hear his voice in my head: *Don't be stupid, Tessa. Don't give your real ID to no one.*

"I'm so sorry," I say, my cheeks flushing from my lie. "My passport and social security card are at home—at my, um, cousin's home."

Mrs. Finneman glances at the purse on my shoulder. "How about a driver's license?"

"I moved here from a city," I say honestly. "I don't drive."

"I see," she says, cocking her head to the side, those shrewd eyes scanning my face. I can't tell if she believes me or not, but I suspect the latter because I'm not a good liar. "Well. I'll need them both by next Friday, or I can't add you to the payroll."

I nod. "I'll remember to bring them."

I don't know what I'm going to do, but I'll talk to Tony, and hopefully he can help me figure out a solution. He never signed on for the job, but he's become my unlikely guide in this strange, new life.

Yesterday, after crying all over him, we packed up a picnic lunch and took Gia to the local beach. Well, *sort of* a beach. I mean, the beaches here are not like the beaches in Jersey with boardwalks and concession stands, roller coasters and umbrella rentals. Here, in Craig, the entire coastline is one long, wild beach, more or less. You just park your truck in the gravel by the side of the road and stroll out onto the "beach." Mind you, there's no soft, warm, cream-colored sand, though. There's mud and debris, seaweed and pebbles.

Not exactly to my taste, though Gia was delighted.

She oohed and aahed over pretty pieces of driftwood, threw rocks into the water, and let Tony teach her how to skip stones. And when a humpback whale and her baby surfaced for air a few yards away? We were there to see it.

After the beach, we went to the local market, where I had a crash course in the Alaskan cost of living.

Mamma mia!

A box of Ritz crackers? Six dollars.

A case of Pepsi? Eight dollars.

A bouquet of hothouse flowers? Twenty dollars.

I never thought I'd miss my local C-Town, but as I strolled down the aisle of my new, local grocer, I had to make difficult decisions about what we could and could not afford on my dwindling savings and modest income. With no more checks from Giancarlo, I'd have to be more frugal.

At one point, I paused in front of the Cheez-Its, which Gia loves, then decided we could get by without them. I reached for a bottle of Starbucks iced coffee before realizing it was ten dollars, then hastily returned it to its spot.

Halfway through our shopping expedition, I had a loaf of off-brand bread, a dozen eggs, generic peanut butter, jelly, ham, American cheese, mayonnaise, chicken noodle soup from a can, dollar pasta, two onions, and four small, dented cans of tomato paste in a small pile at the bottom of my cart. It looked measly and meager, and made me sad, but only for an instant because I was distracted by a commotion behind me.

Tony had started a cart of his own at some point. And every time I put an item back on the shelf, he picked it up and put it in *his* cart. I don't know when Gia convinced him to let her sit in the upper basket, but she swung her legs back and forth, clapping as he reached for a 20-pack of Cheez-Its, and added it to his carriage, which also held two bottles of Starbucks iced coffee, Abby Cadabby juice boxes, Skippy peanut butter, and authentic Italian pasta.

"Hey!" I'd cried. "What're you doing?"

He'd shrugged. "Gia and me's shopping too."

"I can't afford that stuff."

"I can."

"No," I'd told him firmly. "You're already letting us stay at your place. You're not feeding us too."

I'd transferred Gia into my carriage and continued shopping without him, equal parts touched and annoyed that he'd tried to supplement my pathetic purchases.

And in the end, he didn't listen to me anyway.

Damn if there wasn't Starbucks iced coffee in his frig this morning. I don't know how he managed to sneak it by me, but when I shuffled into the kitchen, he poured me a tall glass, and slid it across the kitchen counter with a shit-eating grin.

"I know what happens to Jersey girls when they don't get their caffeine fix," he'd quipped with a twinkle in his eye, then sauntered upstairs for a shower.

I'd smiled to myself, pleased in ways I didn't want to explore.

"Alright, then, Tessa," says Mrs. Finneman, snapping me back to reality, "as long as we're agreed that you'll have your ID here by next Friday, you can start tomorrow. Now, go enjoy your last day of freedom."

We shake hands, and I hurry outside to find Tony and Gia sitting on a park bench side by side, eating ice cream cones like long lost best friends.

"So?" he asks, looking up at me, his face guarded. "How'd it go?"

"I got the job!" I cry.

Gia hops up to give me a one-armed hug around the legs, and Tony winks at me, smiling like he knew I'd be a shoo-in all along. His eyes crinkle with the width of his smile, showcasing a set of deep dimples and bright white teeth.

This man.

I know I've said it before, but it bears repeating again: Madonna, but he's beautiful.

Just like Giancarlo.

But he's not *like Giancarlo!* cries my heart. *Not at all.*

Against all odds and with ample reason to reject us, he has welcomed us to Craig, into his home, and into his life. No matter what happens in the future, I am grateful to him—for his kindness, for his protection, for his help and for his advice.

And not least of all, for his friendship.

"Thank you," I tell him, the words heartfelt and soft. "You're the most amazing friend I've ever had."

As I say this, I'm watching his face, my eyes locked with his, and to my surprise, his whole expression changes. The crinkles around his eyes smooth out. His deep dimples fill in. His lips straighten. He stares down at me for a second before lifting his chin and putting on sunglasses that hide his eyes.

"I better get you two home," he mutters. "Gotta get to a jobsite."

Without waiting for us, he ambles over to his truck, swings his body into the driver's side, and leaves us to follow.

***

Tony

You're the most amazing friend I've ever had.

What. The. Fuck?

I pull out of my driveway, not even waiting for the front door to close behind them.

Friend?

Friend!

Never in my life has a woman—any woman—thanked me for being a… a… *good friend.*

I catch my reflection in the rearview mirror and sneer, feeling utterly disgusted.

I've been thanked for being a good fuck, for giving good head, for designing a spectacular deck, for changing a tire on the side of the road, for—

For being a "good friend"?

"Fuck no," I growl, turning into a gravel driveway. I just built the owner a new dock and the planks need another coat of stain. I park my truck and get the stain and brushes out of the locker I keep in the bed, huffing with anger as I stride in the direction of the hose.

"A good *friend*," I huff, yanking the hose from the house to the dock. I need to clean off the planks and let them dry in the sun before I can start staining. Luckily, it's a nice, sunny day, so it shouldn't take long.

"I don't have women friends," I mutter. "Never have."

I had my cousins, of course, and I guess you could call them my friends, but that's only because we were family. Any other woman on earth was fair game for *fucking*, not *friending.*

Except for Tessa, apparently. She just wants to be friends.

"Ha!" I shout, letting the spray of water wash away a thin film of salt.

Don't get me wrong: Tessa is one hundred and fifty percent not my type. She's too big, too old, and she has too many problems. But, hell, she should still *want* me, shouldn't she?

Fuck, yes, she should. *I* should be the one to gently reject her, not the other way around… not that I want to be with her. Because I don't. Definitely not. Like I said, she's not my type.

But what red-blooded man wants to be friend-zoned? Shit. That's never, ever happened to me, and I don't like it one bit.

Does she think she's such a catch with her thunder thighs and saggy tits? With her plump lips, and those sad, strange, deep brown eyes with long, black lashe—No. Fuck, no. No long lashes. No deep brown eyes. They're plain and boring. She's not even a little bit pretty.

I wrap the hose back up and take a seat on the sea wall, staring out at the water, waiting for the planks to dry.

Not to mention, I think, narrowing my eyes, *her kid's father killed my uncle.*

She doesn't know that, but I do.

And her cousin's still a flaming bitch.

Letting those two facts settle for a second, I ask myself:

What am I doing helping her? Why am I sticking my neck out for her?

The answer is resounding and real: because I've walked in her shoes, and it's terrifying. Not to mention, it's not Gia's fault her father was a douchebag murderer. She's an awesome kid, and those genes sure as shit didn't come from the D'Angelo side, which means that Tessa's responsible for the cool little person she's raising solo.

Tessa.

She's not my type, and yet she's gotten under my skin in the two days I've known her. I like her. I genuinely *like* her, as a person, and thinking back through my relationships with women, I realize that I didn't like that many of them. I like my female family members, but I don't know that I actually liked the women I dated. My previous relationships were, as Theresa surmised, pretty shallow. Built initially on the thrill of the chase, followed by the delight of mutual pleasure, and perpetuated by the pride I felt with a gorgeous girl on my arm, I preferred going to the movies over long conversations, and when they tried to engage me in pillow talk, I'd pretend to fall asleep.

I guess I am *pretty shallow*, I think, tightening my jaw. I dated beautiful women for their looks and for how their looks made me feel. Thinking back on my last two relationships, I realize I couldn't tell you Mandy's favorite cuisine or Rachel's favorite Christmas movie. I never asked. I didn't care. Truth be told, I still don't.

But I can't help wondering if Tessa cooks, and if she does, if she prefers her Bolognese with onions, garlic, and basil as I do, or if she has another twist on gravy that hasn't occurred to me. I bet she does. I bet she puts something weird in it like minced anchovies or bacon. My mouth waters. I'd be down for trying it, I guess, especially if it's Gia's favorite.

My mind wanders, suddenly curious as to whether she's an "Elf" girl, a "Die Hard" girl or a fan of Hallmark Christmas movies? I can picture us sitting together on my basement couch, Gia holding a huge bowl of popcorn between us. We smile at each other over her head, settling in for a warm night of—

Wait.

Stop.

I don't have fantasies about my fucking friend *Tessa.*

Absolutely not.

My dream girl is still out there, and she's barely legal, scorching hot, ready to please, likes onions, garlic, and basil in her Bolognese and happily lets *me* choose the Christmas movie.

I ignore the fact that this alternate vision of my future someone feels flat and one-dimensional in a way that never bothered me before now.

Then I stand up, grab the stain and brushes, and get to work.

***

When I get home a few hours later, my whole house smells like my nonna's kitchen, and I have a funny feeling my curiosity about Tessa's cooking skills is about to be satisfied.

"Hi!" says Gia, greeting me at the door with a big hug around my left leg. She looks up at me. "You smell bad and good at the same time."

I grin at her. "Stain and sunshine."

"It's six o'clock and the sky looks like lunchtime."

"Days are long here."

"I almost tinkled in my pants but then I 'membered where 'the john' is."

"Good for you."

"My mamma's making dinner."

"Oh, yeah?" I ask, still standing in the foyer with her wrapped around my leg, her butt using my Timberland work boot like a seat. "What's she making?"

"Sausage and peppers."

"*Salsiccia*," I murmur, my mouth flooding from the smell of anise and fennel mixed with fried onions, peppers, basil, garlic, and tomato.

"Yeah," says Gia. "She calls it that, too."

"Smells good," I grunt.

"Yeah. She's good at making it. But my nonna's better."

Gia finally releases my leg and hops up, pirouetting around my foyer. Then she flits away, back to the living room where the TV announces that "My Pretty Pony" will be right back.

Sniffing under my arms, I realize that Gia's right. I smell bad. My Zia Marina would have my head if I sat down to a meal of homemade *Salsiccia* smelling like this.

I stick my head into the kitchen, finding Tessa standing at the stove.

"Hey."

She turns around, smiling at me. "Hi!"

"You making dinner, huh?"

"I found sausages in your freezer and veggies in the fridge. Hope you don't mind?"

"Nah," I say. "Smells good. I like *Salsiccia.*"

"It's my dad's favorite," she says. "My mother makes it every other Sunday."

"After mass."

She nods, her expression wistful. "Yeah. Family supper."

My heart clenches for a moment, remembering the hundreds of Sunday suppers I had at my aunt and uncle's house. Despite losing my parents at a young age, my childhood and adolescence had been mostly happy, full of cousins and laughter and extended family showing up for long afternoons of eating and watching the Jets lose another season.

"It smells like home in here," I tell her.

What I don't tell her, is that with her standing at my stove, cooking one of my favorite meals, it *feels* like home, too. It feels familiar. It feels good. Good in a different way than sex or work. Good like a lullaby. Good like a hug. Good like something I lost before I ever knew I had it. Good like something new that I might want to try.

Am I missing my mother? My aunt?

Or is this—I gulp, uncomfortable with the notion, even though it clarifies quickly in my mind—what it looks like to be *friends* with a woman?

Tessa's wearing black leggings and an oversized gray t-shirt that reads "Enjoy New Jersey" in the red Coca-Cola font. Her black hair's piled on top of her head in a messy bun, and she's barefoot with shellacked red toes. While she's not exactly giving me a semi, my gaze slips to her red lips and linger there for a moment before I meet her eyes again. She has spectacular lips and beautiful eyes. No doubt about it.

"I gotta shower."

"Sure," she says. "Dinner's ready when you are."

"That's nice. Thanks."

"It's the least I can do," she says, turning back to her work.

As I leave the kitchen, I find myself warming up to the notion of being friends with Tessa and decide that if it comes with Jersey-style dinners, maybe it wouldn't be the worst thing in the world.

CHAPTER ELEVEN

Tessa

On Thursday evening, I pick up Gia at the Craig CCC after work, and we walk to Freya's FroYo two blocks away. My girl is bubbly and bright, happy and chatty as we walk along, her My Pretty Pony backpack rattling with today's art project inside. We sit down at an outdoor table, and I order our usual: one small cup of vanilla frozen yogurt.

We've been in Craig for almost a week now, and it's just starting to feel like home.

Our routine is fairly simple: we wake up to Tony's pancakes and coffee before bidding him goodbye for the day. Gia and I shower and get dressed. I pack our lunches, and we wait for the 9:26am bus, which gets us to the Presbyterian Church on Spruce Street at 9:48am. I drop her off at the Craig CCC, located on the lower level of the church, and walk two blocks to the library, where Mrs. Finneman is waiting for me. When I leave work at four, I pick up Gia, and we go to Freya's, where I treat her to a small froyo while we wait for the bus. Once home, I make dinner for the three of us, and then we wait for Tony to come home—usually by six—and have dinner together.

After I wash the dinner dishes, Gia and I retire to the basement for the evening, leaving Tony alone to enjoy his home in peace.

I'm anxious about getting on his nerves—about Gia being too energetic or inquisitive—or getting in his way. I get paid every two weeks, and until I've received at least two paychecks, I can't start thinking about moving out. I'm hoping that if we're helpful, but otherwise unobtrusive, houseguests, he won't ask us to leave before I'm able to find somewhere decent to live.

On the bus ride home, Gia asks to sit with her friend, Max, from school, so I'm free to look out the window, thinking about our life here, and the life we left behind.

I haven't spoken to my parents yet, and it eats at me not to be able to talk with them in any real way. Aside from the encrypted email I sent from Tony's account last Sunday, I haven't been in touch with them at all. I know they must be worried. But has Santo been in contact with them? Harassed them? Are they living in a state of fear—for me and for themselves?

And what about my family back in Newark? When I didn't show up for work on Monday, was Francesca frantic? Or had Santo—who expected me at the wake on Friday evening—already reached out to her by Saturday, asking where I was? I say a quick prayer, begging God to look out for my parents and family; to protect them from the D'Angelos.

Tony arranged—via his contact in Florida—to have a set of false IDs made for me. When he confirmed my name,

I have to admit, I panicked… for a second.

"Hey. Are you a Theresa or a Contessa?" he asked me.

"I'm not Theresa!" I blurted out.

"Yeah. Okay. Contessa, then." He grinned at my expression. "You can't blame me for asking. It wouldn't be the weirdest thing for you and your cousin to have the same name. Especially if you were both named after your grandmother, right?"

I had nodded weakly, grateful I hadn't been found out; still worried he'd kick me to the curb if I knew I was responsible for the verbal ass-whipping he received a few weeks ago.

My new IDs—with the name Contessa Ruggiero—should arrive via FedEx next week. I add their cost—six hundred dollars—to the growing debt I owe him, both financially… and emotionally.

Another reason I'm not anxious for Tony to figure out I'm Theresa? I have grown attached to him during our short, intense acquaintance.

It can't be overstated how wrong I was about this man.

I mean, I haven't known him for very long—a few weeks since I read his ad, and a few days in person—and sure, he could still turn out to be a monumental asshole, but the reality is that days of crisis tends to show off someone's true colors more vividly than days in common time, and he's come through for us over and over again in ways I never could have imagined. Going along with the charade of us being family, welcoming us into his home, and offering me invaluable advice about how to stay safe in my new life. Not to mention, the way he makes breakfast for my daughter every morning and sneaks her favorite treats (and mine!) into his grocery cart. Picnics on the beach and ice cream cones in town and learning the channels that show the best children's cartoons.

He's a good man.

He's kind. He's funny. He's protective.

His ad made him sound shallow, but certainly, the way I read his ad was colored by my personal experiences with hot men. Because of the way Giancarlo treated me, I assumed that Tony was cut from the same cloth.

But he's not. Not at all.

Not that he isn't cocky (because he is), but I sense he's worthy of so much more than a fleeting decoration on his arm. If I were to help him rewrite his ad, I'd tell him to concentrate less on the superficial and more on the meaningful. I'd tell him that he's worthy of a *partner*—someone who's capable of loving him deeply and accepting his love in return. I'd tell him that placing a premium on youth and beauty may not serve him well; that both qualities are temporary, and neither represent the depth of which I suspect he's capable.

Then again, maybe I'm wrong.

Maybe I'm overinflating his character because of his kindness to us.

Maybe he's risen to the challenge of our unexpected visit, but despite his valiance, our presence is testing the limits of his endurance.

Maybe he can't wait to go back to his carefree bachelor life, and he's counting down the seconds until we leave.

Maybe he really does want someone beautiful, fun, and young; with or without the chance of a deeper, more lasting connection.

Whatever he wants, it doesn't hurt my feelings anymore that I'm not it. Who am I to judge him? He has been my savior, and my wellsprings of gratitude belong to him. If beautiful, young, and fun would make him happy, then that's what I want for him. In fact, whatever I can do to help facilitate that happiness will be my pleasure. My honor.

Smiling at my reflection in the bus window, it occurs to me that I'm in an ideal position to find the perfect girl for him. The Craig Library is a social hub of sorts. Everyone in town comes in at some point or another—if not for a book or video, then for a community meeting or to use the internet. I make a promise to myself to be on the lookout for someone both deserving of and appealing to Tony. Maybe I can find someone beautiful, young, fun, who's *also* decent and kind.

The bus stops in front of Tony's driveway on Port St. Nicholas Road, and I take Gia's hand, thanking the driver for the door-to-door service.

"Mamma, what's for dinner tonight?"

Gia skips ahead of me, down the gravel driveway, toward the log cabin that's our temporary haven.

"I don't know," I tell her. "Tony's friend is coming over to play cards, so I think we're ordering a pizza."

"Ooo! I love pizza!"

Using the key Tony made for me, I unlock the front door, holding it open for Gia, who bounds into the front foyer.

"Antonio!" she calls. *"Siamo a casa!"*

"Ciao, bellas!"

I hear him in the kitchen and smile to myself. Maybe one day, his wife and daughter will come through the door as we just have and he'll call *Ciao, bellas,* to them just as he has to us. I tamp down any feelings of wistfulness, and double-down on my determination to help him find the perfect someone.

He steps into the foyer, sweaty from work or a run, and grins at us. He's so tall and tan, and his thick, dark, wavy hair glistens. *Dio mio*! For a panty-dampening second, my heart wishes for what I cannot have. (I'm only human, after all.)

"How was work?" he asks me.

"Huh?" I ask weakly, staring at a drop of sweat making its way down the side of his face.

He chuckles at me. "Work? How was it?"

"Work?" I chirp, my senses returning. "Oh! Yeah. Good. I set up the community room for a meeting tonight and helped a bunch of kids with their homework."

He nods at me, then slides his gaze to a waiting Gia. "And you? How was school?"

"Awesome," says Gia, opening the zipper on her backpack and taking out a box made from popsicle sticks. "I made your house!"

Tony squats down, looking at her handmade piece of art. The sticks jut out at imperfect angles and big glops of glue are only half-dry, but Tony reaches for the little model gingerly, like it's precious. He holds it up, and turns it around in front of his eyes, studying it carefully. Gia's hands are fisted by her sides, and she switches her weight from one foot to the other, anxious for his judgment.

"This is… terrific!" he declares, looking up at her with twinkling eyes.

Her little body leaps in the air. *Joy*.

"You didn't make this yourself!" he says, beaming at her excitement. "It's too good!"

"I did!" she insists. "I made it all by myself!"

"Well," says Tony, standing up to his full height and walking over to the sideboard in his foyer. "It deserves a place of honor because it's so awesome. I'm going to put it here, okay?"

Gia dances after him, admiring her little creation as he places it in the center of the table. And it's right about then—watching the two of them—that I realize tears are streaming down my face.

"Gotta go to the bathroom," I mutter, moving past them quickly to head downstairs to the privacy of the basement bathroom. Once there, I sit on the toilet and sob.

My father did his best to be a positive male role model in Gia's life, but he was well into his seventies when she was born. She never had a "father" figure. Giancarlo denied her that crucial relationship. For four years, I've done my best to be everything for her, but it occurs to me that I need to do better. Gia *needs* a dad, and sooner than later, I need to find someone who might be able to fill the position.

"Mamma?"

A little knock on the door makes me stand up and

splash cold water on my face.

"Y-yeah, baby?"

"Tony wants to know what we want on our pizza. I said sausage and onions is our favorite."

"Great job, honey."

"His friend's name is Jim."

"That's nice."

"Can I watch TV?"

I sniffle. "Sure. Down here, okay? Let's give Tony some space before his friend comes over."

"Aw. Tony doesn't mind if I—"

"Do as I say, Gia."

"Okay, Mamma."

A moment later, I hear her turn on the basement TV and look at my reflection in the mirror. With the sun out all the time, I've gotten some color on my cheeks this week, and I could be wrong, but I think this climate is better for my skin than inner-city Newark: my complexion is clearer and smoother. I pull my hair out of its bun and let it fall, inky and wavy, around my shoulders.

Huh. Not bad.

I cock my head to the side, thinking about Gia's need for a father, and wondering about my ability to make some headway in that direction. I mean, girls are scarce around here, right? That should improve my chances with the local male population.

Maybe this guy, Jim, is single.

***

Tony

Tessa flips over her card, locks her eyes with Jim's and purrs, "Blackjack."

Again.

"Sweet Jesus," says Jim, banging his fist on the table and grinning at her. "You're a card shark, lady!"

She chuckles, and it's nothing like her normal laugh; the sound is husky and soft like she's trying to be sexy. She lowers her eyes, peeking up at him flirtatiously from blacker-than-usual lashes. "Not even."

"Tony!" says Jim. "Did your cousin deal cards in Atlantic City or something?"

I glance at Tessa, feeling annoyed. "There's just so much about my little cousin I don't know."

"Ha!" Jim laughs. "Like the fact that she never loses?"

"Oh," says Tessa, winking at him. "I lose from time to time. I just don't like it."

"Well, who does, sweetheart?" asks Jim, staring at her across the table, his ruddy face intensely focused on her. "Deal 'em again."

"Anyone need another beer?" I ask, but Jim's entranced, watching Tessa shuffle the deck, and neither of them respond.

I shove up from the table with a huff and head to the kitchen. Opening the fridge, I stand there for a second, letting the cool air hit my flushed cheeks.

I don't like it.

I don't fucking like it at all.

From the moment Tessa came up from the basement,

dressed in black heels, black leggings, and what can best be described as a black-fucking-*teddy*—a black, lace mini-dress that shows off the swells of her tits like a dream—she's been flirting her ass off with Jim. And fickle, fucking Jim, who seemed so smitten with Rachel last week, is lapping it up like a big dumb kitten sitting in a tub of ice cream.

I grab a beer and grimace, because there's no doubt about it: Tessa can wear the shit out of a sexy outfit. She's dark, sensual, and tempting, and I'm no more immune to her than Jim.

Since she arrived in Craig, I've seen her look bedraggled, dressed conservatively for work in pants and a blouse, and in sweats or pajamas before bed. Until now, I haven't seen her *dressed up*, like for a night out, and fuck, but she looks good. *Jersey* good.

She also did her hair up and put on bronzer, and her lashes are all inked up and black and her lips are plumper, slicker and redder than usual. She's wearing rhinestone earrings and some sort of musky perfume that smells like summer at the beach.

What grinds my gears the most is that she could have chosen to look like that at any point over the past week, but she chose to dress up for Jim. *For Jim,* not for me.

I pop off the cap of my beer and head back out to the deck in time to see Tessa win again. As I open the sliding door, she glances at me over her shoulder, and for just a second, I *see* her. I see the sweetness of her real smile under her sexy makeup, and the gratitude she feels to me for letting her crash here. My heart swells. My—

"Hot damn!" whoops Jim.

She faces him and our moment is gone. And damn if I don't miss it, standing there in the doorway of my own deck like I'm interrupting *them* on a date. And that thought makes me feel mean.

"Tessa," I say. She looks up at me, her eyes wide, no doubt surprised by the edge in my tone. I look meaningfully at Gia, who's sitting on the couch in the living room watching TV, then back at Tessa. "It's Gia's bedtime, isn't it? Or are you too busy flirting to notice?"

Her lips part. "I-I…"

"Tony," says Jim. "Come on."

I don't look at him. I keep my eyes locked with Tessa's.

"I guess I—I lost track of the time," she murmurs.

She looks confused—embarrassed and hurt—which makes up a little for the way she's been coming on to Jim and ignoring me. But it also makes me feel like shit because I didn't mean to hurt her. Or, if I did, I somehow thought it would feel better than it does.

"Well," I say, softening my tone. "It's eight o'clock."

"I guess I should get her to bed," she says, pushing away from the table.

"Jesus, you're such an asshole," mutters Jim.

He's not wrong.

I turn to my friend. "The kid needs to go to bed."

Tessa stands up in front of me, as though protecting me, even though I'm the one embarrassing her.

"Tony's right," she says softly to Jim. "I should get her to bed. And me. I have work tomorrow." She reaches out her hand to my friend. "It was fun meeting you."

"Yeah," says Jim, standing up hastily to take her hand in his. "It was great to meet you, too, Tessa. Maybe we could—"

"Good night, cuz," I say from behind her, my voice clipped.

Jim's eyes meet mine, narrowing for a second before he drops her hand.

"Good night," says Tessa, brushing past me into the house.

I watch through the window as she picks up a half-asleep Gia in her arms and heads for the basement door without a glance behind. Once she's gone, I turn back to Jim, whose eyes, like mine, followed Tessa to bed.

"Gin rummy?" I ask him.

Jim looks pissed.

He's a big guy, and when he puts his hands on his hips, puffs up his chest, and stands up to his full height, he's a bear. He's fucking formidable.

"Do you have a problem with me?" he asks.

"With you? No."

I sit down at the table, gathering the cards together and forming them into a deck.

Jim pauses for a second, grunting in annoyance before sitting down across from me.

"You're kinda acting like a dick."

"Is that right?" I ask him, shuffling the cards.

"Is this, like, some kind of territorial thing? Because she's your family?"

I deal us each a hand. "Honestly, man, I don't know what you mean. It was the kid's bedtime. That's all."

"Okay," says Jim, folding his hands on the table and refusing to play until we hash this out. "Let's try this a different way. I'm going to be direct with you: I think your cousin's very pretty and really fun. I'd like to ask her out on a date. Is that going to be a problem for you?"

Yes.

"No," I say with what I hope is a nonchalant shrug. "It's up to her."

"Okay. Good." Jim picks up his cards, his shoulders finally relaxing. "Maybe I just read the situation wrong. It seemed like…"

"Like what?"

"Honestly? Like maybe you were into her, and you didn't like me paying her so much attention." He makes his cards into a ham-fisted fan, then looks up at me. "But that would be pretty weird and kinda gross, considering you two are family." He holds my eyes. "So, like I said, maybe I read the situation wrong. Maybe you're just protective of her."

"That must be it," I say.

"I can respect that," Jim assures me. "But you know I wouldn't treat her bad."

I know.

Jim's a decent guy. In fact, if one of my *real* cousins was here with us now, I'd give Jim my blessing to ask her out. But Tessa's *not* my cousin, and the thought of Tessa and Jim hanging out makes my stomach hurt.

"Yeah, I know," I say, picking a card. "But I thought

you were into Rachel. What happened with that?"

"Am I allowed to be nice to Rachel and still ask your cousin out on a date?" Jim scoffs. "I mean, you were *dating* Mandy and Rachel at the same time."

Yeah. But neither Mandy nor Rachel was Tessa.

"So?"

"So, Rachel and I *aren't* dating," says Jim. "She's clearly still interested in you. I may as well go out with Tessa and see if we click."

You click, I think sourly. *I saw you clicking for the past hour.*

"Fine," I mutter. "It's between you and her. I'll stay out of it."

"Good," says Jim. "Then we're agreed. I'll swing by the library tomorrow and see if Tessa wants to go out for dinner this weekend, and you'll stay out of it."

I can't look up at him. If I do, he'll see it in my eyes—how much I dislike this plan.

"Yeah. Whatever," I say, discarding one card and picking up another. "Now can we stop talking about chicks and fucking play?"

Jim chuckles and nods. "A hundred percent."

Two hours later, Jim's gone, and I'm standing at the deck railing, looking out at the harbor, finishing the last of my beer in the twilight. When the door behind me slides open, I glance over my shoulder to find Tessa standing in the doorway.

She's wearing gray sweatpants and a loose black t-shirt. Her hair is piled on her head in her standard messy bun, the bronzer's been scrubbed from her face, and she has glasses on. I didn't know she wore glasses, and something inside of me tightens. It's like she's sharing a secret with me. And, damn, but I like the way she looks in them. A million naughty librarian fantasies take root in my dirty mind.

"Hi," she says softly.

"Hey."

I sigh, turning back to the water. She still smells like summer when she joins me, resting her elbows on the railing beside me. I breathe in deeply.

"I'm not a bad mom," she tells me.

Fuck, I'm a piece of shit for making her feel bad.

"I know that."

"I don't let guys get between me and Gia."

She doesn't deserve criticism on her parenting from someone like me.

"You're a *great* mom, Tessa," I say. "I know that. I can see it. You gave up your whole life to come here and keep her safe. I never met a mom as good as you."

"Then… why were you—?"

"Being such an asshole?" I ask her, my eyes holding hers for a moment too long before sliding to her lips and resting there. "You looked good tonight. Hot."

She scoffs, her eyebrows shooting so high they almost disappear into her hairline. "Me?"

"Yeah, you." I bite my bottom lip, punishing it for what it wants as I turn away from her, gazing back out at the moonlight on the water. "You're not ugly, Tessa. You're… you know, good-looking."

"You think so?"

I grin at her. "Definitely. Especially when you dress up."

"Oh, yeah?"

"Fuck, yeah," I murmur, looking down at her, at her pretty face turned up to mine, bathed in moonlight. *I could kiss her. I could kiss her right now…*

She turns away from me suddenly, breaking off our eye contact and looking back out at the water.

"But I'm not young, I'm not thin, and I've got a kid."

All true.

"A *great* kid," I tell her.

"Yeah," she says with a soft chuckle. "Thanks." She's quiet for a moment before adding. "She *is* great, but she needs a dad."

Oh.

Oh my God.

I see.

I suddenly see tonight in a different light: the way she dressed for Jim, the way she flirted with Jim. She's looking for a man. She's looking for protection. She's looking for safety. She's looking for a husband to take care of her and be a dad to her little girl. Because she's a phenomenal mom who'll do anything to keep herself and her daughter safe.

"Jim seems like a good guy," she says.

"He is. He's a really good guy."

"Any kids?"

"No," I say. "But he's an uncle. Talks about his sister's kids a lot. He loves them."

"That's good."

Is it? Is it good?

Why doesn't it feel good?

"Yeah. Jim's solid." I finish off my beer in a long swig and decide I should do something nice for her to make up for being an asshole earlier. "He's going to stop by the library tomorrow and ask you out."

"Oh, yeah?" she says, her voice lilting, like this is good news. "That's nice."

I raise the bottle over my head and throw it into the growing darkness, listening with satisfaction as it shatters on the low-tide rocks.

Is it? Is it nice?

Why doesn't it feel nice?

"Night, Tessa," I tell her, heading back into the house alone.

"*Buona notte*, Tony."

I glance back at her through the window before I head upstairs—at her short, round form in the moonlight—and hope that walking away from her tonight without kissing her isn't a decision I'll regret forever.

CHAPTER TWELVE

Tessa

A book appears in front of me on the counter, a manicured hand resting on top of it.

I look up into the face of a young, pretty woman with shoulder-length, strawberry-blonde hair and bright green eyes.

Maybe… mid-twenties? Hmm. A possibility for Tony?

"Just this?" I ask her.

She smiles back at me, sliding her library card across the counter. "Yes, please."

Rachel Morehouse.

I scan the card, making a mental note to go back and look at her personal information later. I won't learn much, but I'll be able to tell if she has a spouse or children sharing her library account.

I take a second look at the book and realize she's borrowing *Archer's Voice* by Mia Sheridan. It's one of my favorites.

"This is a good book," I tell her. "I've read it about a million times."

"Really? I love a good romance."

"Then you're in luck," I say. "This one will knock your socks off."

She cocks her head to the side. "You read a lot of romance?"

I nod. "Yeah. A ton."

"You know what you should do?" she asks. "You should make a display shelf with romance recommendations. They do that in bigger libraries."

"Oh, I don't know—"

"You should!" she insists. "And maybe we could start up a book club too!"

"A book club?" I've never belonged to a book club, let alone started one.

"You know," she says, "like, we all read a book on our own, then get together to discuss it. We had a book club here a few years ago and it was so fun. Mrs. Finneman even let us bring wine and cheese to the meetings."

"Really?"

"Yes!" cries Rachel, her enthusiasm contagious. "Think about it. I could spread the word around town if you decide to go for it."

"I'll definitely give it some thought," I say, sliding the book back to her.

The front door across from the circulation desk opens, and I look up in time to see Jim Kerrigan step inside.

"Jim!" I exclaim.

"Hey, Tessa," he says, grinning at me as he approaches the desk. "How're you doing?"

"Great. I enjoyed our game last night."

"Me too," he says, his face pinkening under his bushy red beard.

I watch his eyes slide to Rachel, widening in recognition, lingering on her face.

"Oh, uh, hey, Rachel."

She looks surprised to see him. Why? Because he's in the library? Or because we know each other? Whatever the reason, she recovers quickly, offering him a warm smile.

"Hi. Jim."

He flicks a quick glance at me, then back to her. "How's your dad doing?"

"He's okay," she says. "I know he's looking forward to seeing you this weekend." She turns to me. "Jim's coming over to watch the Hawks play with my dad."

"How nice."

I smile at her, then look back at Jim, who's still gazing at Rachel.

Huh. There's a not-so-subtle current between these two. I can feel it.

"Well," says Rachel, glancing back and forth between me and Jim. "I guess I should be going."

"See ya, Rachel," says Jim, watching her go.

He finally turns back to me. "Hi. Again."

"Hi, again," I say, my hopes for Jim dashed. I changed my tune after Giancarlo and promised myself that I wouldn't let the next guy treat me like shit. I don't date guys who are pining for someone else. And Jim is definitely pining for someone.

"So... I was wondering—"

"What was that all about?" I ask, resting my elbow on the counter and cradling my chin in my palm.

"What do you mean?"

I raise my eyebrows. "You and Rachel."

"Me and… Rachel?" He flattens his hands on the counter near my elbow and acts all confused, like he has no idea what I'm talking about. "Nothing! I mean… nothing at all. We're friends. I, uh—she looks after her dad, and sometimes I—"

"Jim," I say, patting one of his hands gently, "you're lying. To yourself, or to me. Which one is it?"

He sighs. "I don't *want* to like her."

"But you do."

"I *wish* I didn't."

"But you do."

He puts his hands on his hips and nods. "But I do."

"So why were you about to ask me out when you should be asking *her* out?"

"She's not into me."

That's not what I saw, I think, but I don't say that. I wait for him to finish.

He grimaces. "She used to date Tony, and…"

Ah. This pinches my heart, though I wish it didn't. Rachel and Tony would make a really attractive couple, and she seemed nice, suggesting we start a book club, and taking care of her dad.

"Yeah," continues Jim. "And I get the feeling she's still into him, you know?"

"I get it," I tell him, scratching at a speck on the

counter like it's my life's mission. I don't want Jim to see my eyes when I ask: "Is Tony still into her?"

"No. Not at all."

I look up, and I can feel myself smiling. I know I'm supposed to be Tony's cousin and all, but I'm happy to hear that he doesn't want to be with Rachel. I can't help it.

"He doesn't like her father and with Rachel, her father's part of the deal."

My eyes narrow. "What if her father wasn't in the equation?"

"Nah." Jim shrugs. "I just don't think he's into her. She's pretty, but I don't think she's his type."

Interesting. "What *is* his type?"

"Someone more like you," he says. "At least, I think." He shrugs. "He's always talking about the girls from 'back home.' They're hotter. They're funnier. They take better care of themselves."

"We're *not* cousins," I blurt out.

Jim raises his eyebrows, but then surprises me by nodding. "Huh. I wondered."

"*What* did you wonder?"

"I got a weird vibe from you two last night." He grins at me. "Why pretend you're related?"

"Long story," I say. "My cousin met Tony first. And then the Websters gave me a ride to his house and—"

Jim holds up his hands. "You already lost me. But it doesn't matter. Like I said, I picked up on something last night. Tony was intense about you. I think… I think he's into *you.*"

"What? No! No. Definitely not." I laugh, but my cheeks heat up. I pluck a book from the Returns basket and check it back in. "No way. I'm not his type at all. I'm fat. I'm almost thirty. I have a kid."

Jim screws up his face at me like I'm crazy. "You're not skinny, but you're not fat either. Whatever your age is, you look great. You're *really* pretty, Tessa. And Tony couldn't stop talking about your daughter last night."

"Really?"

Jim holds up his hands. "God's truth."

"Huh. Okay."

We stare at one another for a second before Jim cocks his head to the side. "I have an idea. And I don't know if it's a good idea or a bad idea, but…"

"Lay it on me."

"Well…I have a thing for Rachel, right?"

"Clearly."

"And Rachel has a thing for Tony."

I'm not so sure about that, but…

"So you say."

"And Tony doesn't have a thing for Rachel, but he *might* have a thing for you. Hell, *you're* the exact kind of girl he's always talking about."

I'm not so sure about that either, but…

"I'm following you…"

"Well, what if you and I *pretended* to date. Like, pretended to get together and be a couple. I'd come pick you up for dates, and you'd be dressed up all pretty to make Tony jealous. And you'd call me while I was over at Rachel's house this weekend so I could show her what awesome boyfriend material I am…"

"So…use each other to get what we want?"

Jim blinks at me, his grin widening. "I knew it! You *do* want Tony."

Fuck. I do?

Yes, I do.

My cheeks blaze with heat. Suddenly, I can't check in books fast enough. I grab for one, staring at the computer, away from Jim.

"What? Ha! No, I don't. Well, I mean… I mean, who wouldn't? But no. He's out of my league. I'm not… I mean, I'm not what he—"

"Not what he wants?" asks Jim. "Tessa, he doesn't *know* what the hell he wants. That's the truth. He talks about meeting some hot, young girl—he even placed a personal ad looking for someone—but I watched him go through a bunch of responses. The only girl who appealed to him was some chick named Theresa from Newark. He talked to her for a week over text and he was, like, over the moon for her. Singing around his house. Walking tall with this shit-eating smile. He hadn't even met her in person yet, but he was on cloud nine. Whoever she was, *she* was what he wanted."

He has no idea what his words mean to me. I stare at him, hoping he'll say more, my heart thrumming in my chest, painful and wonderful all at once.

Jim shrugs. "Anyway, she was from Jersey… like you."

Just like me.

"Okay," I say. "I'll do it."

"You will?"

I nod. "Sure. I'll ask Tony to babysit tomorrow night. Pick me up at seven?"

"Babysit? Oh, man. That'll pour some salt in the wound." He chuckles. "Will do. And you'll call me at Rachel's on Sunday?"

"Absolutely," I tell him, offering my hand so we can shake on our deal.

***

Tony

Know what I love about Fridays?

Everything.

Even in Alaska, where there aren't as many places to party as there are in New Jersey, or—for crissakes—New York City, there's this unparalleled feeling of freedom when you finish the workday on a Friday afternoon.

Time to burn. Time to relax. Time.

I love it.

And to add a hit of awesome to my already awesome mood, my house smells like good, old-fashioned Italian food when I open the front door. Tessa's cooking. And her mini-me welcomes me home.

"Antonio!" yells Gia, running into the front foyer barefooted. I love it that she calls me "Antonio." I thought I left that name behind forever when I left Bayonne, but Gia's single-handedly resurrected it. *"Ciao, come stai?"*

"Va bene, bambina!" I cry, lifting her off the ground. "How was your day?"

"Va bene!" she exclaims, cupping my bristly cheeks in her little hands. "Mrs. Robinson says it's going to get cold soon. But that's crazy."

I chuckle, swinging her back down to the ground. "Why is that crazy?"

"Because it's summer."

"Yeah," I say, hanging up my jacket in the closet, "but it gets colder quicker here. By Halloween you'll be wearing a parka."

"Will I still be here for Halloween?" she asks me, her eyes wide and excited.

My smile falters.

I don't know how to respond.

My instinct is to declare, *Of course you'll still be here, silly! You and your mom will still be living here with me. Your mom will still be making delicious Italian food for dinner, and I'll take you Trick or Treating and—*

"We'll see, honey."

I turn around to find Tessa standing in the kitchen doorway. Her dark eyes, which are so very pretty, connect with mine, and I feel a *zap!*—a jolt of something sudden and shocking—deep inside.

Gulping softly, confused as to what I'm feeling, I give her a half-smile. "Dinner almost ready?"

She shrugs. "It could simmer a while more. I made Chicken Cacciatore and a melanzane di Parmigiana that's staying warm in the oven."

My mouth waters.

Chicken cacciatora and eggplant parm? Dio mio.

"Smells amazing."

She grins at me. "I hope it will be. I found some chianti. Want a glass?"

Fuck, yes, I do.

But I'm also smelly, and aside from the fact that my Zia had rules against sitting down to dinner *alla brutto*, I want to—I don't know… I guess I want to treat Tessa and her cooking efforts with respect. I want to sit down at her table, showered and shaved. I want her to know I appreciate her work.

"I should shower first."

She nods. "Yeah. You should."

"Wiseass."

"Takes one to know one," she throws over her shoulder as she walks back into the kitchen, calling to Gia to help her set the table.

She's fucking sassy sometimes, Tessa, and I fucking love it.

I take the stairs two at a time, pulling my shirt over my head and unbuttoning my jeans before I hit the landing. I turn the shower to hot, then finishing undressing in front of the bathroom mirror, checking out my naked body before the steam hides it.

I'm a good-looking man.

Tall, muscular, and tan, I'm also hung. My cock is long and wide, and I've never gotten any complaints about how I use it. I started fucking when I was fourteen years old. I've had most of my life to perfect my technique.

I love the sound a woman makes when she comes—the

moaning, the little cries—the way her body writhes when my tongue laps at her clit or my cock hammers her pussy. And the sighs—the fucking sighs of satisfaction when I shoot my load, filling her with my hot cum? Yeah. I miss that. I miss that bad.

I'm stroking my dick as these thoughts slide through my mind, and hard as a rock by the time I step into the shower. I squeeze some shower gel into my hand and brace my forehead against the slick tile, jacking myself off as I think about making love to a woman. I picture my lips sliding up her naked leg, my head nestling between her thighs as my mouth works her slit. After she comes the first time, I slide my meat into her hole, and when I lean down to kiss her mouth, I'm kissing…

Tessa.

Wait. What? Fuck!

I try to switch the face to Rachel… to Mandy… to fucking *anyone*, but it's a no-go. The face I see, that I'm actively jerking myself off to now, is Tessa's. So, I lean into it, God help me. I let it happen.

In my fantasy, her eyes close, but my tongue is still in her mouth, tangling with hers, and her warm, soft body is taking my cock to the hilt, her full tits rubbing against my chest, her moans turning into cries turning into these loud, intense screams of—

"Ahhhhh!" I groan, opening my eyes to find I'm coming in creamy spurts against my shower wall.

I rest my palms against the slick tiles and close my eyes again, picturing Tessa's eyes closed, her lips bruised and red, in a perfect "O" of pleasure. I'm panting and sated, exhausted and invigorated. We fucked hard in my mind, and we both loved it.

The water cools for a second, indicating someone downstairs flushed the toilet, and I'm zapped back to reality. My eyes pop open and I back away from the wall, the evidence of my ardor already sliding down the drain.

Tessa. Huh. Do I think about Tessa like… like that?

Apparently, I fucking do.

I reach for the shampoo and scrub it into my head a little too hard, like I'm angry with myself.

Tessa's not my type, is she? I mean, she's… she's fat. And she's definitely over twenty-five, and she's—

I don't give a shit.

She's pretty.

She's still in her twenties.

And sure, I used to think a chick with a kid was bad news, but that was before I met Gia. Gia's a gamechanger.

I rinse off and grab a towel, drying my body as I head into the bedroom. Pulling on boxer briefs and a clean pair of jeans, I think about having Tessa in my home over the past week. I've liked having her here. I like her company. I like *her.* And if five minutes ago in the shower is any proof, I'm attracted to her, too. *Wildly* attracted.

Blood rushes to my cock.

I hope the kid goes to bed on time tonight.

***

Dinner is delicious, of course, but afterward, because it's a Friday, Tessa lets Gia watch a movie and stay up a little late.

That's okay. I've cooled off by now. I'm just enjoying their company; the way they make my house feel more like a home.

We sit outside on the deck, side by side at the picnic table, facing the harbor while the kid watches TV in the living room. And it's nice. It's *so* fucking nice.

Not for nothing, but I'm so aware of Tessa beside me, now that I've had dirty fantasies about her. She smells good, and I like the sound of her voice. I like listening to her talk and that's a first for me.

"I was wondering if I could email my parents again tonight?"

Her parents have written back to her three times since she contacted them last week. They've been asking where she is and if she's safe, and begging her to write back and tell them what's going on.

"Sure," I tell her, sipping my wine. "But keep it brief again. As brief as you can."

"I will," she promises. "I just want them to know me and Gia's safe and they don't need to be worried."

"Don't tell them where you are," I warn her. "No references to the weather or distance or anything like that."

"I know," she says, sighing softly. She takes a sip of her wine before asking, "I wonder if the D'Angelos have been bothering my family in Newark."

"You can bet they are," I tell her, the words slipping out before I can think better of them. But there's a reason none of my family lives in Jersey anymore. There's a reason they all left. Santo made it uncomfortable to stay.

"You had dealings with them?" she asks. "The D'Angelos?"

How much should I tell you?

"Yeah," I mutter, taking another sip of wine.

"How bad?"

"Bad," I tell her.

"Did you… did you know Giancarlo?"

I purse my lips, placing my wineglass on the table behind me. "Yeah."

"How well?" Her voice is getting thinner with emotion.

"Tessa," I say, "you don't want details."

"Yeah, I do," she says, twisting to face me. "I *need* details. I need to know what's coming."

"Nothing's coming for you," I growl, my eyes meeting hers. "You hear me? Nothing."

"Tell me, Tony," she begs. "Please."

I take a deep breath and let it go slowly. "We're hiding from the same people, you and me. Just for different reasons."

"Did Santo kill your parents?" she asks me in a whisper.

"No," I tell her. "He killed my uncle."

She gasps, her hands flying up to cover her mouth as her eyes widen. "Wh-what?"

Gently, I pull her hands from her face, holding them in mine. "My uncle was in charge of Bayonne, just like Santo and Vito are in charge of Newark. They wanted to expand their territory. My uncle was in the way."

"Oh, my God."

I raise her hands to my lips, closing my eyes as I kiss

her skin. "Shhh."

"I'm so sorry," she murmurs.

"It was three years ago," I tell her, my lips nuzzling her flesh.

"That's when you came here."

"Santo and Vito like to be sure there're no leftovers. No witnesses. No retaliation. I could've been a problem for them."

"—if you'd avenged your uncle's death."

If…

My eyes pop open and I raise my head to look at her.

"But I didn't." I say it slowly, though part of me burns with shame that I didn't say anything, do anything, take action.

She searches my face, and I wonder if she's calling me a coward in her head. The thought chills me, hurts me, makes me feel empty.

"What are you thinking?" I whisper, afraid to hear her answer.

She tugs her hands away from mine, and for a second, I think she's going to call me a *vigliacco* again. I brace myself for it as I would for a smack, squinting my eyes and turning my head away from her.

But Tessa surprises me by reaching for my face, just as Gia did earlier in the foyer. She cradles my face, looking at me earnestly, locking her eyes with mine.

"I'm thinking you've lost a lot of people who were close to you… who you loved. I'm thinking of how sorry I am that's happened to you. I'm thinking of how brave it was for you to let us stay here. I'm thinking—"

My lips land urgently on hers, stealing her words and her breath.

When you expect someone to hurt you and they surprise you with sweetness instead, what the fuck else are you supposed to do?

I kiss her gently, which surprises me after the passionate way I fantasized about her earlier. I nip at her bottom lip first, then her top. I sweep my tongue across her lips before sliding it into her mouth. She meets me with hers and they glide against each other, hot and wet, slinging little bolts of lightning from my mouth to my groin where my cock twitches, ready to spring into action. And that's exactly where I hope we're headed when Tessa suddenly pulls away from me.

Her tits rise and fall from the speed of her shallow breathing. She stares at me intently for a second, her dark eyes severe in the dying light.

"I need a favor," she says, dropping her hands from my face.

"Anything," I tell her, and in that second, I mean it.

"Can you babysit for me tomorrow night?"

Cue the sound of a needle scratching brutally across an old-fashioned record.

What the—WHAT?

"I'm sorry," I say, because I can't be understanding her correctly. We just kissed. We were kissing. We could have gone on kissing all night, or we could have put the kid to bed, gone up to my room, and fucked all night until dawn.

But instead, she's asking me to… "What?"

"Babysit. Tomorrow night," she says, still panting softly from our kiss. She angles her body away from mine, looking out at the harbor. "For Gia."

I stand up and put my hands on the deck railing, feeling about five times as gutted and twenty times as stupid as when her cousin verbally lambasted me. These women are… *diavolas*.

"Jim asked me out," she's saying, "and I don't—"

"I don't want to hear about it," I tell her curtly. "Stop talking and I'll do it. I'll fucking babysit. Just shut up."

"Thanks," she says from behind me. I hear her stand up and step over to the door. It opens, but she pauses to say something else: "Hey. I didn't mean to hurt your feelings. That was nice. I just—"

"Please stop talking," I growl, refusing to look at her.

"I'm sorry. I… Good night," she says softly, stepping inside the house and closing the door behind her.

And me? Soundly rejected for the first time in my life?

I stare out at the harbor, feeling like shit, and wondering what the fuck I did wrong.

CHAPTER THIRTEEN

Tessa

It took everything—every ounce of self-control and self-esteem and pride and hope—for me to pull away from Tony while he was kissing me last night. I could've kissed him all night long. I could've happily given myself to him, legs spread, eyes rolled back in my head until morning.

But then what? When he woke up in the morning and looked at me like he made a mistake? What then?

I can't risk it. I won't.

This time, I'm going to be smart. This time, I'm playing for keeps. This time, I'm not going to let myself be used and dumped.

Gia needs a dad.

I'm sick and tired of being lonely.

And we both need protection.

So, voila! God sends me Tony, and you know what? Against all odds, he ticked my boxes: Gia adores him, we have a common enemy and he's sworn to keep us safe. Besides… I *like* him. I like him a lot. I like him a lot more than I ever liked Giancarlo, and I had a *kid* with him, for crissakes.

So, yeah. I'm aching for Tony to fuck the living daylights out of me. And after that sweet, hot kiss last night, I'm primed for more. But I'm not going to be stupid. I'm not going to blow this. Not yet, anyway.

Gia's sitting at the kitchen counter eating waffles when I step into the kitchen on Saturday morning. She greets me with her usual enthusiasm, but Tony's cold, giving me an icy glance before looking away.

"Do I smell coffee?" I ask timidly.

He gives me a look, then takes a mug down from the cupboard, placing it on the counter with an angry *thud.*

Okaaaaay. He's still pissed about last night.

As I pour myself a cup of coffee, I can't decide if this is a good or bad thing. Maybe good? That he feels so strongly about what happened? Or bad… because he'll tell us to get out of his house? I take a sip of coffee, letting it scald my throat, and hoping like hell I'm not overplaying my hand. I need Tony. I want Tony. But a guy like Tony has to work for me, suffer a little for me, or I won't matter to him.

"Can I use your laptop?" I ask.

At once pouty and dismissive, he gestures to his upstairs office with a flick of his wrist. I roll my eyes as I head up the stairs.

He's not speaking to me?

Men are such babies.

His office smells masculine—of soap and leather, clean laundry and the spicy aftershave he wears. I sit down in his desk chair, logging into the desktop and waiting for it to connect to Wi-Fi. Clicking on the ProtonMail icon, I wait a moment for the account to come up, enter Tony's password, and then click on the Inbox.

I'm startled to see that there are four new messages from my parents, and all of the subject lines are in caps: YOUR FATHER, GET IN TOUCH, RE: YOUR FATHER (2), and PLEASE WRITE BACK. A chill races down my spine as I click on the first message, sent sometime yesterday.

Tessa, your father had an episode this afternoon. We're going to the ER. I'll write back later and give you an update. Please call ASAP. We're scared. We love you.

I scramble to click on the next message.

In the waiting room, but the ER doc thinks it was a small heart attack. Right before your father collapsed, he got a call from Santo D'Angelo. Do the D'Angelos have anything to do with why you left NJ? GET IN TOUCH with me ASAP, Theresa mia.

I click the next message, my heart in my throat.

Your father's in surgery, getting a stent. Madre de Dio, why haven't you called? It is cruel of you not to be in touch. We are scared out of our minds wondering where you and Gia are. Your Aunt Carmela is here with me, thank Jesus, so I'm not all alone, but my daughter should be here with me. You're breaking my heart.

Tears stream down my face and my hands shake as I click on the fourth and final message.

Your father survived the surgery and is in recovery.

My eyes slide to the date and time the message was sent, but I can barely see the words through my tears.

"What happened?"

I jump in Tony's chair, surprised to hear his voice. Looking over my shoulder, I find him standing in the doorway, his face softer than it was in the kitchen this morning.

"Your shoulders are shaking," he tells me, crossing the room to stand beside me. "What happened?"

"My—my father," I manage, sniffling through tears. "He had a—a heart attack!"

"Jesus."

"I have to call them!" I cry, reaching for the cordless phone on his desk. "I have to!"

He places his hand over mine, pulling it away from the phone. "No."

"Tony!"

"No!"

"There must be a way!" My brain is spinning, trying to figure out a way to get what I want, what I need. "How come you could text with me?"

His eyebrows furrow. "What? When?"

"I-I mean… with Theresa? You texted back and forth. How did you do that?"

"I used a burner phone," he explained, his face relaxing. "And besides, I've been Tony Silvestri, in Craig, Alaska, for three years now. There's no trace of Antonio Silva anywhere anymore. He disappeared into thin air. I'm a ghost. I'm as good as dead. They've stopped looking for me, or at least I think they have. You've only been gone for a week. You gotta stay low. Off the radar. Hidden."

"But Tony!" I wail. "My dad's sick! Please!"

"You *can't* use the landline," he says firmly, squeezing my hand in his. "But I'll go to town and get you a burner phone."

I stare at him with watery eyes, my tears still falling at a clip. "You will?"

He nods. "But Tessa, you can't—*you cannot*—use the landline. You'll put us both in danger if you do that. Tell me you understand that, or I can't leave you alone."

"I won't. I promise."

"Write back a quick message over email. Tell them you'll be calling on a burner, but they can't ask where you are."

I nod, jerking my head to the rhythm of my sobs.

Tony looks at our joined hands, seeming to realize that he's still holding mine.

"Sorry," he says gruffly, releasing me.

I miss the warmth and safety of his hand immediately. So much so that I have to tightly clasp my hands together in my lap to keep from reaching for him, for demanding the solid security of his hand holding mine once again.

"I'll be back in fifteen minutes," he says.

The lump in my throat makes it impossible to respond, so I nod, more tears staining my cheeks as his footsteps head down the stairs.

***

"Keep it short. Give nothing away," he coaches me, his eyes severe when he hands me a nondescript, clamshell phone.

I nod, taking the phone and dialing my mother's cell number.

"Theresa?"

"Mamma!"

"Oh, Theresa, *mia bambina*! Where are you? What happened? Are you safe? Your father is here. He's sipping juice. How is our Gia?"

My mother sobs into the phone, telling my father in Italian that I'm calling, although I'm sure he already knows.

"Mamma, I can't talk long."

"Is it true, Tessa? Is Giancarlo D'Angelo Gia's father?"

"It's true, Mamma."

"Que vergogna!"

I ignore this. I can't deal with her feelings of shame right now. I have too many other things on my plate.

"Mamma. Focus. We're safe. We're hidden. We're somewhere far away."

"Where are you? As soon as your father can travel, we'll—"

"No!" I cry. "You stay put. You can't help us. And you could lead the D'Angelos to us!"

"*Va bene.*" She's silent for a moment, then says: "We're so worried, Tessa."

"I'm sorry for that, Mamma. But we're safe here. That's all that matters." I gulp. "How's Pappa?"

"He's doing better today. One more night in the hospital and he can come home. *Grazie a Dio*. Your Zia

Carmelina is driving me crazy."

I smile sadly, thinking of these two old ladies rattling around in a rural Italian hospital. "I'm sorry I can't be there."

"Take your own advice and stay put," my mother says, then adds, with steel in her voice: "Don't you dare let the D'Angelos get to her."

"I won't, Mamma." My eyes brim with tears. "Tell Pappa I love him."

"*Ti vogliano bene*, Theresa."

"I love you too, Mamma."

"Kiss Gia from *Nonna e Nonno*."

"*Lo prometto*," I whisper, hanging up the call.

I swivel around in the chair and look up at Tony with watery eyes. He drops to the floor and pulls me off the chair and into his arms. Cradling me on his lap, he strokes my hair as I cry against his shoulder, wetting yet another of his t-shirts with my snot and tears. I owe this man a load of laundry for sure.

"I'm a t-terrible d-daughter," I choke out.

"Nah," he says. "You're brave and strong. You're doing your best to be a great mom."

"My m-mother's all alone in—in Italy. She's sc-scared."

"You can't live her life for her," he says gently. "We all make choices. She chose to go back to Italy. You chose to come here to keep Gia safe."

"And them! I'd die if Santo hurt them!" I cry. "I—I needed to d-disappear. For all our s-sakes."

"And you did," he assures me. "You're hidden here."

"Santo called my d-dad! That's what b-brought on the

h-heart attack."

"You knew Santo would call your parents eventually," he says, still running his hands over my hair. "But they have no idea where you are. They can't help him. He'll figure out they're a dead end and leave them alone."

"What about my f-family in Newark?" I ask, leaning back to look up at him.

"They don't know where you are either."

"But Santo could hurt them. Squeeze them. He could make life difficult for them if he thought they were withholding my location."

"If they don't know anything, he'll sense that, and he'll eventually move on."

"Are you sure?" I ask, sniffling pathetically.

"Once my aunt and cousins moved away from Bayonne, the threats stopped," he says. "What's the point of hammering away at a bunch of people who have zero idea where you are? He'll eventually give up, right? It's common sense."

But you weren't hiding his granddaughter.

The thought makes a chill slide down my spine, despite Tony's strong arms around me. But I take comfort in his words. They're all I have.

I lean away, looking at his tear-splotched shirt. "I'm going to do some laundry for you today."

"Fuhgeddaboudit," he tells me with a slight shrug.

"You sound like you're from Jersey," I tell him.

"You weren't sure before now?" he asks, a smile teasing at his lips. He reaches up to dry the last of my tears with the rough pads of his thumbs. "How about some breakfast?"

My heart swells with affection and gratitude, yes, but something else, too. Something more. Something that feels suspiciously close to… love.

Love?

No. Not really.

Gratitude. Affection. Attraction.

Yes, yes, and yes.

But love? That would be impossible after so little time, wouldn't it?

And yet, when I look into his beautiful face, so close to mine, so full of concern and compassion, it's all I can do not to claim his lips with mine and profess my undying devotion.

He puts his hands under my arms, lifts me gently from his lap to the floor, then stands up. "I'll make you some pancakes, okay?"

"Your pancakes are going to make me as big as a house."

"I don't mind," he says. "I think I like a little meat on the bone."

My cheeks flush. "Is that right?"

He winks at me, and my heart skips a beat.

"Come down when you're ready."

***

Tony

I'm sitting next to Gia on the couch watching some Disney movie about a fuzzy blue dragon with an attitude, when the doorbell rings.

Muttering to myself in annoyance, I glance over at the basement door, waiting a beat to see if Tessa appears, then get up to answer the door myself.

Jim stands on my front stoop dressed up in—*get this*—slacks and a blazer. Slacks. And a fucking blazer. Like he's going to the high school prom or something. I didn't even know he owned anything dressier than flannel.

"Hey, bro," he says, offering me his beefy hand.

I consider not shaking it, then take it at the last minute. "Hi."

"Can I come in?"

"Whatever," I say, stepping aside so he can enter my house.

"Tessa here?"

"Whadda *you* think?"

Jim glances over my shoulder, looking for her.

"Getting ready, I guess."

"Yeah," I growl bitterly. "For your hot date."

We stand there in my foyer, eyeing each other, and I realize I'm sizing Jim up as I would my competition. And what do I see? Well. He's tall and strong, overweight, but not too fat. Muscular as fuck. His red hair is neatly combed, and he's trimmed his beard for tonight.

I guess if Tessa's looking for a super-sized Raggedy Andy doll, she could do worse.

I cross my arms over my chest. "How's things?"

"Since Thursday?" he asks. "Fine."

"So… if you're going to be dating my cousin—"

"She's not your cousin," says Jim. "She told me the

truth."

"Oh, she did, did she?"

"Yep. She met you through *her* cousin."

I don't know what to say. I was going to act all protective and give him a list of rules, starting with Tessa's goodies being off-limits, but that potential conversation has now disappeared into the ether.

"Don't try anything," I tell him anyway.

"Like what?" he asks, all innocent.

I step closer to him. "Be nice. Be decent."

He gestures to his stupid blazer. "Do I look like someone who wants to show her a bad time?"

"Don't show her too good a time either!" I half yell, half snarl.

"Tessa's a grown up," he points out. "I'm sure she can decide what she wants and what she doesn't."

She doesn't fucking want you, I think, remembering the way she kissed me back last night, the way she melted into my arms on my office floor this morning.

I hear the basement door open and close behind me and look over to see Tessa standing against it.

Fuck. Me.

Starting at her shoes, I check out her shiny, black stiletto heels, my eyes tracing up her legs, which are covered in slick, black material that looks like patent leather. She's wearing a baby doll top in crimson silk, that clings to her breasts, underwire forcing them up and out, so they pillow just over the black lace edge of the bodice. Around her neck, she wears a silver chain with "Tessa" spelled out in rhinestones, with similar baubles dripping from her ears. Her lips match the color of her blouse, her eyes are smoky and dark, and her hair is gathered high on her head, with some falling around her shoulders too.

She's fresh to death tonight. For *Jim*. And I fucking hate it.

"Hey, Jim," she purrs, coming closer to us, her shoes click-clacking on my floor.

My mouth's hanging open.

I can feel it, but I don't give a shit.

She looks hot. So. Fucking. Hot.

And suddenly I'm thirsty as shit.

"Close your mouth, Tony," she says, giving me this sexy fucking wink. "I'll be back at…" She looks over at Jim, who's grinning at her, and shrugs. "… later."

Then she takes his arm and lets him lead her to the car like she's the fucking queen of the fucking Nile.

And me? I'm left behind.

To fucking babysit.

***

Three hours later, Gia's sound asleep on her cot downstairs and I'm drunk from too much vodka on the rocks. True fact? As the minutes tick by, and Tessa's still out, I want to drink more. I want to be dumb fucked up by the time she gets home. I don't want to hear her invite Jim to join her downstairs. I don't want to think about what he's doing to her when it should be me down there with her.

With a bottle of coconut Stoli under my arm and a glass of ice in my hand, I head upstairs to my home office.

Everyone on the planet has a social media footprint, right? If I can't be with Tessa in person right now, I can sure as fuck troll her Facebook account, because that's not creepy, right?

I log into my laptop, watching as one of the more expensive programs I found scrambles my location, bouncing my IP address off hosts in Eastern Europe and finally settling in Hawaii. For the first time since Tessa landed on my doorstep, it occurs to me that I don't actually know her last name. Huh. That's weird.

But she introduced herself by way of her cousin. And it's not like I ever demanded to see her passport or anything.

Let's see… if her father and Theresa's father are cousins, her last name could be Rinaldi. Either that, or I could search for her cousin, Theresa Rinaldi, and see if she and Tessa are Facebook friends. If they are, I can find her that way.

I enter the name Theresa Rinaldi, expecting to see a picture of her cousin come up, but my eyes narrow when the third entry on the screen bears a picture of… Tessa and Gia.

I click on the account, opening the profile of Theresa (Tessa) Rinaldi, of Newark, New Jersey, whose cover photo is of Tessa, Gia, and two older people, whom I assume are Tessa's parents.

In my head, something pings. Something she said recently. This morning, in fact.

How come you could text with me?

With… *me*.

"No," I say aloud, scrolling through pictures of Tessa and Gia living their best life in Newark, the last post almost two weeks ago, the day before she arrived on my doorstep. "No."

"You're Tessa, not Theresa."

But picture after picture proves me wrong.

"You're not… *Theresa*," I whisper.

But she is.

Her voice echoes in my memory, and I'm furious with myself that I didn't recognize it before now.

There are plenty of nice girls who aren't as hot as… as… as me. And maybe they have kids and maybe they have baggage and maybe they didn't have the money for braces and maybe they can't afford Gucci and maybe, just maybe, they're just doing their best. Their. Very. Fucking. Best. And then you come along and place an ad like that, and you make them all feel like shit. Like total and complete shit… I've known guys like you all my life, and I just—I just—you know what? You're not a good person, Tony. And you know what else? You don't deserve someone like me!

Holy shit.

Bitchy, hot Theresa and chunky, mom Tessa are one and the same.

Stunned, I sit back in my chair, staring at the screen. There's a picture in the left column that shows half a dozen young women, dressed up to the nines, standing in front of the Wildwood Beach boardwalk sign. I lean closer and recognize the original "Theresa," whom I discover, by flicking the cursor over her tagged face, is actually named "Rosemarie Rizzo."

Tessa used Rosemarie's picture to catfish me, which makes me furious.

But my heart softens when I consider it was *Tessa* with whom I texted. It was Tessa who first resonated for me, who got my heart thumping, who had me singing "Maria" around the house, who made me dream about a happy forever spent with a Jersey girl, here in Craig.

Then again, it was also *Tessa* who screamed at me over the phone, making me feel like total shit, and heaping on my shoulders the sins of Giancarlo D'Angelo.

I get it. She was hurt by him.

But I didn't deserve her anger.

Or did I?

When I think back to our week of texting, I realize how much I talked about her looks. I asked for a picture and called her hot and told her she could be a model.

Maybe I did deserve her anger to some extent. Maybe I did place too high a priority on her looks. And maybe that did, inadvertently, make her feel like shit.

But she lied to me.

She lied about who she is.

She insisted she was Theresa's cousin, when she is, in fact, Theresa.

She had some balls to come here seeking help and protection, when she was also the person who'd verbally torn me a second asshole in a bid to exact revenge on a guy she assumed was exactly like her ex.

If I wasn't so pissed, I'd be impressed.

Fuck her.

(She's phenomenal.)

Fuck her and her lies and her tears and her date with

Jim.

(I wish it was me out with her right now.)

I pour myself a full glass of vodka and shoot it like I haven't had a drink in weeks. And then I have another.

And another.

And another.

CHAPTER FOURTEEN

Tessa

Tony's nowhere to be found when I get home from my date with Jim, which consisted of us having dinner at a local place called The Craig Inn, followed by a *Wonder Woman* double feature at his house to ensure I got home as late as possible.

I check on Gia first, making sure she's sound asleep on her cot, then head upstairs in bare feet to pour myself a glass of water. Wondering where Tony is, I go upstairs to peek into his bedroom, but his bed's empty. I pad down the hall, opening the door to his study gingerly in case he's sleeping.

He's slumped in his office chair, snoring like a bulldozer, with a half-empty bottle of coconut Stoli on his desk. *Okaaaaay. Someone got their drink on tonight.* I grab a blanket off the back of the easy chair in the corner and drape it over his body, which is when my hip nudges the mouse on the edge of the desk, and his laptop blazes to life.

My heart stops for a second as I recognize the pictures illuminating the screen.

Me and Gia at Wildwood.

Me and my Rizzo cousins at the shore last summer.

Me and Rosemarie grinning for the camera.

Fuck.

Fuck, fuck, fuck.

He knows.

He knows who I am. He knows I'm the same Theresa who gave him a verbal beating a few weeks ago; the woman he still refers to as a "bona fide, cold-blooded bitch" in my presence.

I wince, thinking about how he pulled me into his arms this morning, cradling me against his chest, assuring me that everything would be alright. And his face when he told me he likes a little "meat on the bone"? Like maybe he's falling as hard for me as I'm falling for him?

I step away from his desk, clenching my hands together.

Maybe he could forgive me for bringing Giancarlo's daughter to his home—we're both victims of the D'Angelos, after all—but how can he forgive me for verbally crucifying him without cause? There's no way. It was a vicious, unwarranted attack.

"Liar…"

My eyes fly open, and I crane my neck to look into Tony's face, but he's still sleeping. He's dreaming… or having a nightmare about me, more likely.

"You're a fucking liar…" he murmurs, shifting slightly in his chair.

I am, I think. *I'm a fucking liar.*

I came here seeking help and protection I had no right to. And Tony, who I'd so badly wronged, offered it freely and without expectations. My heart squeezes painfully as I realize that the kindest man I've ever known, aside from my father, probably hates my guts now. I close my eyes against the burn of tears, clenching my fists by my sides in frustration.

You're a bad person, I think. *A shitty person.* You're *the user that you painted Tony to be.* You're *the villain in this scenario, not him.*

Backing out of his office with tears of shame and regret streaming down my cheeks, I hurry downstairs to the basement, pulling out our suitcases and throwing our clothes inside. Using Tony's landline to place a call to Jim, I ask if he can come and pick us up. Then I pull our packed suitcases out to the driveway, gather my sleeping baby into my arms, and stand outside to wait for Jim.

***

Sunlight streams through the windows of Jim's spare room, hitting me squarely in the eyes. When I blink them open, I'm face to face with a mounted moose head that's been relegated to the floor before being hung up over the bed.I let out a little shriek as I remember where I am and why. And then? Regret crushes my chest like a brick, and I struggle to take a clean, deep breath.

Sitting up, I notice that Gia's still sleeping in a ball beside me. A glance at the clock on the bedside table tells me it's a little after six o'clock, which means I got about four hours of sleep. I slept for shit, tossing and turning for those paltry hours, Tony's betrayed face haunting my dreams.

After Jim picked us up, and we got Gia settled in the spare room bed, he poured us two glasses of whiskey and I told him everything: first seeing Tony's ad in the *Odds Are*

Good magazine, and texting with him for a week under false pretenses. How I sent my cousin's photo in place of mine, purposely leading Tony to believe I was a hot, young, unattached twenty-something. I told him about our phone call—the one in which I eviscerated Tony, and where my anger came from; about Giancarlo: how he supported Gia financially but refused to acknowledge her as his child. I explained Santo's position in the mob world of northern New Jersey and how he had instantly recognized Gia as his granddaughter at Giancarlo's funeral. I had no other option but to run away, and I had nowhere else to go but Craig.

"He hates me now," I told Jim. "How could he not?"

Jim hadn't seen thing as direly as I. "Because he cares about you."

"Not anymore," I'd sobbed, draining my whiskey.

"I wouldn't be so sure."

"How can he ever trust me again?"

Jim had taken away my glass without refilling it and looked me dead in the eyes. "You'll have to apologize. And you'll have to earn back his trust. But Tony… he's a good guy. I actually think—if you explain everything to him as you have to me—he'll get it. He'll understand."

"He won't," I'd moaned, cradling my head in my hands.

"He might."

"He can't."

"Well," said Jim, "you'll never know unless you try."

Then he'd put away the whiskey and insisted that I get some sleep.

Pushing off from the edge of the bed, I open my

suitcase and take out a pair of leggings and an oversized t-shirt. The shirt reads, *Suns out, Guns out*, in hot pink on black and looks far more cheerful than I feel. After I pull on some furry black boots, I glance at Gia. Knowing she'll be frightened to wake up in an unfamiliar place, I gently wake her up.

"Baby? Hey, baby…"

"Mamma?"

"Morning, sweet girl. Guess what!"

"What?"

"We're having a sleepover at Mr. Jim's house! Isn't that fun?"

"Mr. Jim's house?"

"Yeah! Fun, right?"

"Yeah. Okay," she murmurs, drifting back to sleep.

I grab my purse and head downstairs, not surprised that Jim's also up. His business isn't open on Sundays, but it opens at seven every other morning of the week, so he's likely in the habit of early mornings.

"Coffee?" he asks.

"Yes, please," I tell him.

He pours me a cup. "Then what?"

"I was thinking of going to mass," I say, adding in a sour tone, "for my sins."

"Services at seven and ten on Sundays."

"Can I borrow your truck?"

"Sure." Jim nods. "What about the munchkin?"

"She'll sleep until seven, at least," I say. "I woke her up and told her we had a sleepover last night, so she won't be confused."

"Can I give her some eggs?"

I smile in gratitude. "Thanks. She'd like that."

"What about Tony?"

"I'll go talk to him after church," I tell Jim, exhaling a deep breath. "I'm taking your advice. I'm going to tell him everything. Apologize. Throw myself on his mercy."

"If I know Tony, he'll grant it," says Jim.

"I wish I was as certain as you."

"He likes you," says Jim. "Told me to treat you decent last night."

"The line between Madonna and whore is no joke for Italian men," I tell him. "And I've fallen from grace."

"To piggyback on your Madonna reference, at the end of the day, you're still a mother," Jim points out. "And you're still trying to keep your kid from harm's way. He'll see that, just like I do."

Jim's probably right about that, but what's really breaking my heart right now, is that any chance of Tony seeing me as a romantic prospect is probably gone now. It's one thing to treat a woman in trouble with kindness. It's another to want her in your life romantically. I can't believe there's any chance that Tony could still be interested in me. My chances with him, which were always slim, have now shrunk to non-existent. And it hurts. It hurts so bad because I think he could have really and truly made me happy. We could've made *each other* happy.

Jim holds up his truck keys. "Good luck?"

"Thanks," I say, but I know the truth.

I've been a bitch and a liar.

Luck can't help me now.

Only God can.

***

Tony

My head throbs as I enter St. John by the Sea, but my heart hurts worse, if that's possible.

When I woke up this morning, Tessa and Gia were gone.

Their stuff was packed up and the blankets they were using downstairs had been neatly folded. At some point, I'd been covered up with a blanket, too, which leads me to believe that Tessa—pardon me, fucking *Theresa*—was in my office, saw her Facebook profile up on my screen, and knew she'd been found out.

So, she left. Like a big fucking coward. She left.

Who's the vigliacca now, Theresa?

I cross myself, then slide into a back pew, bowing my head like I'm praying, but I'm not.

I'm pissed.

And worse, my fucking feelings are hurt.

And even worse than that, I'm fucking worried about them.

Where'd they go? Where are they now? Are they safe?

The door to the church opens and closes behind me, and an older couple heads down the aisle together, arm in arm.

Seeing them makes my heart ache in a way I don't

expect. They're frail and small, both of them gray-headed, but the way they lean on each other is so natural, so easy, like they been doing it their whole lives.

Since losing my birth parents at such a young age, and losing my adoptive parents a few years ago, I haven't felt bound to anyone. I haven't felt like I belonged to anyone or like anyone belonged to me. Except…

Except maybe I was sort of feeling a little possessive of Tessa and Gia, now that I think about it. And maybe I was feeling okay—no, not just okay… *good*—about that. I got attached to them in the short time they stayed with me. *Really* attached. Maybe I even started to care for them in ways I never even saw coming.

Maybe that's why it hurts so much that Tessa's a bitch and a liar; and instead of talking to me about everything, she ran away in the night like a criminal.

The church doors open again, but no one walks down the aisle, so I look over my shoulder to see who's entered. And standing there, against the double doors, with her eyes locked on the back of my head… is Tessa.

She raises a trembling hand in hello, her eyes wide and uncertain.

"Get over here," I mutter, furious with her, even as my heart thuds with relief and… joy. *Joy*. Pure, real joy just to see her face again. Theresa "Tessa" Rinaldi makes me ridiculously happy, even when she's driving me crazy.

She slides into the pew beside me, making the sign of the cross and bowing her head.

"You can't hide behind God," I tell her.

"I'm praying," she whispers.

"For forgiveness?"

"Uh-huh."

"Because you're a big, fat liar?"

Her neck snaps up and fiery eyes meet mine.

"Oh, no," I warn her, immediately recognizing my misstep. "You don't get to take that out of context and feel insulted. You *know* I'm attracted to you."

"Big and fat," she grouses. "That's what I am."

"You're not skinny," I agree, "but whatever you're selling, I'm buying. So shut up about it."

She takes a deep breath and sits back in her seat. "You pissed at me?"

"Very."

"I figured." She stares straight ahead at the crucifix hung over the altar. "You want me and Gia to leave, right?"

"Wrong."

Her head twists toward me, her eyes searing the side of my face. "Wrong?"

"Wrong." I turn to meet her gaze. "But first, I need to know what's been true and what's been lies."

She sits back in the pew, finally leveling with me. "My name is Theresa Rinaldi. I'm twenty-seven. I'll be twenty-eight in November. I read your ad in a magazine during my lunch break at my cousin Francesca's salon. After years of Giancarlo fucking me on the sly and four years of him not acknowledging his daughter, I wanted revenge on a hot, cocky guy. I tried to take it on you because of your ad, but it didn't work. I felt like shit for the way I spoke to you on the phone; the way I tricked you into liking me with my cousin Rosemarie's photo. A couple of weeks went by. Giancarlo was shot. Santo recognized Gia as his granddaughter at the funeral, and I left town an hour later. If I had joined my parents in Italy, Santo woulda tracked me down. I had nowhere else to go. So, I came here. To you. Even though I had no right." She gulps softly, looking away from me for a second before seizing my eyes again. Hers are watery now. Full of tears. "You're *nothing* like Giancarlo. You've been good to us since the second we got here. I can't—I can't tell you how sorry I am for tricking you, for how I treated you on the phone. I'll regret it the rest of my life. I'm… I'm sorry, Tony."

She has no idea what hearing this lump confession does to me, because yeah, she's tricked me and lied to me, but hearing it all at once, I realize that none of it is *that* bad. None of it is a deal-breaker. If she wants me anywhere near as bad as I want her, we can still belong to each other. The thought makes my heart soar. It makes a lump rise up in my throat. It makes me feel hopeful after feeling so hopeless this morning when she vanished.

"That's it? No more lies? Nothing more to tell me?"

She blinks her eyes, her lips pursing. "One more thing."

Shit. "Are you married?"

"What? No!"

"Then, what? Spit it out."

"I have no interest in Jim. We're just using each other to make you and Rachel jealous."

"Ha!" I chortle so loudly, old Mrs. Michaelson in the

front row turns around and "tsks" at us.

"He'll be at Rachel's place later watching the Hawks with her dad. I'm supposed to call him so he can show her what great boyfriend potential he has."

"You only went out with Jim to make me jealous?" *It worked.* I chuckle softly. "You're a piece of work."

"I'm sorry," she moans. "I'm really, really sorry. For everything. For all of it."

"Part of me wants to throttle you—"

"Then, I'm glad we're in public."

"—but I want to kiss you more."

She gulps again, lifting her chin, her lips parting in invitation.

"What're you waiting for?" she whispers.

"For one," I say, tracing her lips with my eyes, "we're in church and mass is about to start."

"True," she breathes, her voice low and soft.

"And two, I drank half a bottle of vodka last night and I haven't brushed my teeth yet this morning."

"Oh—"

"But after this," I tell her, tucking my index finger under her chin and forcing her to look at me, "we're going back to my place, I'm brushing my teeth, and then I'm fucking you bowlegged, baby." I search her eyes. "Okay with you?"

Her lips wobble. Her tongue darts out to wet them before she smiles. "Yeah. Okay with me."

The organist sits down and starts playing a hymn.

My hand finds Tessa's on the pew between us, and I

entwine my fingers through hers, squeezing gently.

***

After I take communion, I walk back up the aisle and out the front door of the church, unable to wait any longer to have her. Tossing a glance over my shoulder, I see she's followed me, quietly heading to Jim's truck and starting the engine. She waits for me to pull out of the parking lot, then follows me closely down the long road from Klawock to Craig.

My body's humming with anticipation.

I haven't had sex in months and I'm itchy to get inside of Tessa.

I bet she's wet and warm and soft. I bet she feels like heaven.

Darting a glance at the rearview mirror, I see she's wearing sunglasses, so I can't read her face. By all accounts, which were many since he was a well-known manwhore, Giancarlo D'Angelo was a decent lover. He had a reputation for leaving the ladies satisfied.

How will I compare? I wonder, narrowing my eyes. *Has she had any lovers since him? And if so, how well will I compete with them?*

Shifting in my seat, I glance up at her again, checking out the fullness of her lips, the plush softness of them. I know how they feel beneath mine and my body tightens in response. My foot falls harder on the gas as we approach Craig, as we get closer to my bedroom.

She pulls behind me in the driveway, hopping down from Jim's truck and grinning at me.

"You weren't in a rush, huh?"

I let my eyes drop to her breasts, then slide them back

to her face. "You blame me?"

She puts her hands on her hips, tilting her head to the side. "Fair warning, Tony: I'm not looking for casual. I did that. I hated it."

"I don't want casual neither," I tell her, thinking I wanted to kill Jim last night just for taking her out on a date. I crook my finger and gesture to her. "Come here."

"And we're a package deal, me and Gia," she says, taking a small step closer to me.

"Aw, really? And here was me, ready to send the kid back to Jersey alone."

She takes another step. "I mean it."

"I know you do," I tell her, looping my arm around her waist and pulling her closer.

"I thought you were going to brush your teeth before you kiss me," she says, looking up at me, those dark eyes wide and liquid.

I cup her ass cheeks with my hands and yank her against me. I want her to feel my erection. It's hard and long, straining against my jeans, desperate to invade her cunt.

"You want me," she half-moans, half-whispers, wonder softening her eyes.

"I want you... *bad*."

She bites her bottom lip. "So quit talking and take me already."

She makes me smile, this woman.

"Get naked and get in my bed," I tell her. "I'll join you in a minute."

"Don't make me wait too long," she says, all saucy.

I squeeze her ass, then let her go, watching as she disappears into my house.

Following her inside, I move slowly, letting the anticipation build and grow between us. I wish I had the time (and the self-control) to take a shower first, but I tell myself we can take one together later. I slip into my bathroom through my office and brush my teeth carefully, then splash some aftershave under my arms.

I take off my t-shirt and flex. *Looking good.*

Toeing off my shoes, I leave them by the tub and unbutton my jeans. I'm commando today, so there's nothing between me and the world except for some broken-in denim. Pushing open the door to my bedroom, I freeze at the sight I find:

Tessa lies tits down on my bed, knees bent back, completely naked except for her furry black boots, which she scissors above her back in slow motion.

Propping her chin on her hand, she looks up at me and grins.

"Hey, there."

"*Fuuuuck*," I sigh, leaning against the doorway, my whole body flushing with admiration.

"Good?"

"Fucking fantastic," I whisper.

Her ass is round and full, and her tan skin is smooth and perfect. She's littler like this, without her oversized t-shirts and tight leggings covering her up. Her hips are wide, her legs are stubby, and she's—*somehow*—the sexiest thing I ever seen in my life, and exactly what I never knew I wanted.

She's vulnerable, lying ass up like this, but she's also confident, and it's an awesome combination.

"Why are your pants still on?" she asks me, a teasing smile tugging at her lips.

I unzip them, shoving them over my hips and carefully pulling them up and over my erection. My cock is visibly pulsing, impatient to feel her.

She raises her eyebrows. "Is that for me?"

"You want it?" I ask, shucking my jeans from my ankles and standing tall and proud before her.

"I want it in my mouth," she says, her eyes dancing, but her voice gravelly. "I want to suck you off before you fuck me."

All for making her happy, I step forward, positioning my cock in front of her lips.

"Tony," she says, looking up at me, "You've been good to us."

"You're welcome," I say, my voice gruff and raspy. I'm staring down at her; at the tip of my erection about a centimeter from her delicious lips, and I think it's the most erotic thing I've ever seen.

"You saved our lives."

"Happy to help."

"I want to show you how grateful I am," she says, licking the length of my cock from top to bottom, then from bottom to top.

"Uh-huh. Yeah. Good."

Her tongue teases the head, swirling around the lavender skin, which strains to fill her mouth.

"You were here for me," she says, making another long lap up and down my shaft, "when nobody else was."

"Oh," I groan, my legs feeling weak.

"And I'll never forget it," she finishes, taking my entire length down her throat as her tongue somehow still manages to flick against the base of my cock.

She reaches behind me, her nails digging into my ass as I pump into her mouth. When I'm on the brink of coming, she pulls back, teasing the tip of my cock with her tongue before forcing my meat back down her throat again.

I growl with satisfaction, plunging my hands into her hair, entwining the silky strands through my fingers. "Jesus! Tessa!"

When I look down, her lips are taut around my thick cock, her eyes dark and lusty as she takes me deeper and deeper with every thrust.

"I'm gonna… shit! I'm gonna… Ahhhhhh!"

She squeezes my ass brutally, her nails drawing blood, and I come like a geyser, spilling my seed down her throat, and struggling to stay upright as I climax. My cock convulses in waves as my body trembles with the force of my orgasm. I forget where I am, who I am, what time it is, but never for an instant do I forget who's doing this to me. It's Tessa. Theresa. *My Theresa.*

♫ *Theresa! I just met a girl named Theresa!* ♪

Music thunders in my head as I ride out the waves of ecstasy.

Mia donna. My woman.

I'm shaking and breathless when she slowly eases her

lips up the length of my cock, landing a sweet kiss on the head before planting her elbows on the bed and looking up at me.

"How *you* doin'? she asks me with a satisfied grin.

I fall forward on the bed beside her like a downed tree.

"Ah… maaaaaazing," I sigh.

She sits up and I hear her boots fall to the ground. A second later, she's lying on her back beside me. And because I've already come once, strong and hard, I find I want nothing more than to return the favor before we get to the business of fucking.

"Spread your legs," I command, my voice rough from my recent grunts and groans of pleasure.

"Okay."

"Knees up."

She obeys.

I maneuver myself between her legs, running my lips from the crease at the back of her knee to the crease between her thigh and her cunt. I nuzzle her there for a second, feeling her adjust her body a little under the scratch of my beard.

"Want me to shave real quick?" I murmur.

"You better fucking not," she answers quickly, making me chuckle.

Gently spreading her lips with my thumbs, I stare at the erect, red button of her clit for a second, admiring the perfectness of it. I read somewhere once that a woman's clit has more nerve-endings than a penis. That blew me away and gave me a better appreciation for the importance of eating pussy. I made sure I knew how after that.

With a slow, long stroke, I lick her exposed pussy from top to bottom, repeating the motion several times. She's already warm, but she's hotter and redder when I lean back and look down again. Her body writhes and I grin.

"More?" I ask.

"Stop. Fucking. Around," she tells me, and I lean close to her, chuckling, my lips vibrating against her magic bean.

"As you wish."

I lick up, down, and around the clit, increasing the pressure of my tongue with each pass, and listening to her moans build to cries. She writhes beneath my mouth as I suck her clit lightly then let it go, laving my tongue around the dark red bud to soothe it before sucking it between my lips again.

The sharp, long nails that razed my ass are in my hair now, pulling and twisting, her obvious pleasure making my cock harden all over again. Her cries build and build until she's a decibel away from screaming, and then I clasp the back of her thighs, burying my face in her cunt as I finish her off. Her body bucks off the bed with the speed and strength of her orgasm, her head thrashing on my comforter, her thighs tight, then loose, tight, then loose, shuddering and shaking against my shoulders as I pant against her.

Gently, slowly, I lean away from her, straightening out her jelly legs on the bed and sliding two fingers inside her body. She floods them with cum, opening her eyes in time to see me put them in my mouth, licking them clean.

She's ready.

"Fuck me," she sighs, her voice soft but firm. "Fuck me now."

Kneeling on the bed, I pull her closer to me, lining up my hard cock at her soaked pussy. I want to be slow when I take her, when I join our bodies together for the first time, but I can't. I want her too badly. I need to feel her. I need to know—in this moment in time, if not forever—she belongs to me, and I belong to her.

"You're mine," I tell her, easing my fat cock into her pussy.

When I'm inside to the hilt, my full balls flush against her ass, she opens her eyes.

"I'm yours," she pants, reaching for my face.

As I thrust back and forth into her body, she kisses me madly, her tongue finding mine and swirling around it, excited mewls and moans riding from the back of her throat and tickling my lips.

I come quickly, shuddering with the force of my second climax, emptying my balls into her pussy, and sighing with satisfaction as she takes my load with low-sounding moans of pleasure. I'm not sure if she came until I open my eyes and look at her face. Her lower lip is still snagged between her teeth and her eyelids flutter with an orgasm of her own.

Collapsing beside her, I pull her back against my chest, marveling that I've fucked many, but none of them hold a candle to my Tessa.

"Fuck, yes," I groan, anchoring my arm beneath her breasts and pressing my lips to the back of her neck. "You're the best I ever had, baby."

She draws my hand to her lips and kisses it before placing it back under her breasts—her gorgeous breasts, which I haven't even begun to explore yet. I hold her tighter, feeling fine.

"That was good," she whispers. "That was so, so good."

"Come home," I say, kissing her shoulder. "I don't want you two at Jim's. Come back here, okay?" I nuzzle her gently, adding again, "Come home to me."

"Yeah," she murmurs, her voice shaky. "Okay."

"Hey," I say, rolling her to her back and looking down at her face. Tears fill her eyes. "What? What is it?"

She sniffles, her face still flushed from our lovemaking.

"Home," she says with a little sniffle. "You called this home."

"*Your* home," I tell her, leaning up on my elbow and pushing away her tears with my thumb. "For as long as you want it."

"I want it," she says. "Thank you."

"Share my room," I tell her. "We'll put Gia's cot in the office."

"Yeah." She nods, reaching up for my face and pulling my lips down to hers. "Okay."

We make love twice more—again in bed, and once in the shower. When she leaves to go get Gia and return Jim's truck, I dry off and change into jeans. We'll have to wait for round four until the kid falls asleep tonight. I can't fucking wait.

After I bring Gia's cot up from the basement and make

it all pretty in the office, I sit down at my laptop and open an internet session. There was a deep web chat board I used to check out regularly when I first left New Jersey, to see if anyone was looking for me. Though I haven't logged into it for months, I decide to take a look at it now.

Narrowing my search to "Black_Angel_NJ," the handle of Santo D'Angelo, my worst fears are confirmed. He's offering $350,000 to anyone who can lead him to Theresa "Tessa" Rinaldi and/or Gia Rinaldi, last seen deplaning at the Ketchikan Airport. There's a grainy, black and white security camera photo of the girls with their Juicy suitcases. It's them, alright.

A chill goes down my spine.

He's closer than I thought.

I log off quickly, narrowing my eyes as the screen goes blank.

Over my dead body will he find them.

CHAPTER FIFTEEN

Three Months Later

Tony

"Popcorn's ready!"

I sit down on the couch with a waiting Gia, who's wearing snowflake pajamas and a reindeer antler headband with blinking red and green Christmas lights on the tips. She reaches into the massive bowl on my lap for a handful of buttery perfection.

"C'mon, Mamma!" she yells through chomps of popcorn. "We're ready!"

"Yeah, Mamma!" I yell, winking at Gia. "It's movie time!"

We hear Tessa's footsteps on the stairs, and I look over in time to see her appear—all five-foot-three inches of the fiery woman who's become my entire universe these past few months. My heart races with pleasure to see her. With happiness.

Whatever joy I knew as a child was lost to me when my parents died, and whatever fleeting happiness I knew living with my aunt and uncle, was always undercut by the notion that they were family, yes, but they weren't *my* family.

With Tessa and Gia, I'm relearning the meaning of family: what it means to have one, what it means to belong to one, what it means to know you'd sacrifice anything—even your own life—to keep them safe and happy.

Tessa stops in front of the couch, putting her hands on her hips and grinning.

"Well, aren't you two a pair!"

"Me and Tony's like peanut butter and jelly," says Gia with a giggle.

"Then I'm the bread," she says, "squeezing you two in a big hug."

She's right, I think, gazing at her with an emotion I've recently identified as love. She's what holds the three of us together.

"Where do I sit?" she asks me.

I'm tempted to point to my lap with a suggestive smirk, but instead, I make room for her on my other side.

"Next to me, baby."

She sits down beside me, her hip pushing into mine as she gets comfortable, resting her head on my shoulder. I hit play on the remote, then stretch my arms along the back of the couch, creating a safe harbor for my girls.

As the theme song to "Elf" plays merrily and we see baby Buddy crawl into Santa's bag at the orphanage, I reflect on my feelings for Tessa. I don't have a lot of experience with love; not the romantic kind, anyway. I loved my parents. And I loved my uncle. I still love my aunt and cousins, and I probably love Big Jim in my own way. But loving a woman is different, and for me—at thirty-two years old—I'm experiencing that love for the first time in my life.

It was back in November, on Thanksgiving, when I realized my feelings for her with clarity. Tessa insisted on hosting the Websters, Rachel and her father, Big Jim, his sister, brother-in-law and their kids for a huge Thanksgiving dinner: thirteen people around a makeshift table that extended from my kitchen to living room. I sat at one head, and she sat at the other, and when she asked everyone to bow their heads so she could give the blessing, I felt it. It was as clear and honest as any other visceral feeling I've ever had: *I love you. I belong* to *you,* with *you. Please, Tessa, don't ever leave me.* When I murmured "Amen," it was to my silent prayer, not hers.

Since then, I've been coming to terms with my feelings, day by day, in a thousand different ways. I've also been considering what I want to do about them. I know me and Tessa's only known each other since September, but the truth is, when you know, you know.

I know.

I don't want anyone else. Ever.

I want her. Forever.

I don't have a ring yet, but I could order one. I could ask her on Christmas Eve, or Christmas Day, or New Year's Eve. I still have a few weeks to pick my perfect moment. I only know one thing for sure: I want Theresa Rinaldi to be my wife by next year. And I want to give Gia half a dozen brothers and sisters if that's okay with Tessa.

"Are you even watching?" Tessa whispers near my ear,

sucking the lobe between her lips for just a second.

"Are you trying to distract me? Because I'm glad to haul your ass upstairs if that's your goal."

She chuckles, and it's this sexy, throaty sound I fucking love. "Behave yourself. We're watching a movie. With a minor."

I laugh with the girls as Buddy gives an angry raccoon a hug and arrives in New York City to the tune of "Pennies from Heaven." Tessa oohs and aahs, telling Gia all about her favorite Christmas spots as Buddy visits them on the TV. I have good memories of New York, too. But lately, my East Coast connections have been haunting me.

I go online for about ten minutes every night to see if there are any developments in the search for Tessa and Gia, and from what I can gather, Santo combed Ketchikan for my girls, with no success. Bearing in mind that Ketchikan is served by thirteen seaports and has flights departing for all over the world, he had to settle on a strategy and stick to it for a while. He must have decided to concentrate on air travel instead of focusing on the various ferry destinations.

Assuming the girls would try to elude him by hiding in a larger city, he sent teams to Anchorage, Fairbanks, and Juneau, but those guys have been searching for three months and coming up dry. The reality is that there are dozens of towns accessible by road from Anchorage and Fairbanks. He has a lot of ground to cover, and the locals tend to be closed-lipped about their neighbors; especially when a stranger is asking questions.

My hope is that when too many trails go cold, he'll

eventually give up.

It all comes down to how determined Santo is to find them, and how much in resources he can put toward the hunt. I stay armed, but for now, at least, I'm confident that my girls are well-hidden. I hope so, anyway. I hope it with every breath I draw.

"Dad!" yells Buddy at a bewildered James Caan. "It's me! Your son! Buddy!"

I chuckle along with the girls, squeezing them tightly and vowing to keep them safe.

***

"You've never cut down your own Christmas tree?" Jim asks Gia, who's taking a ride on his burly shoulders as he treks through the snow. "That's crazy!"

We're tromping around the woods, outside of town, where Jim promised the best Christmas trees can be found. And afterward, Rachel's meeting us at my house for tree trimming, a chili dinner, and "The Polar Express," on my downstairs TV. Jim and Rachel are on the brink of becoming an "item," and watching them find their way to each other has become one of Tessa's and my favorite pastimes.

"*Nonni* always got our tree from the gas station on the corner."

"The gas station?" exclaims Jim. "Christmas trees don't grow at gas stations!"

"Yeah, but they sell them there."

I keep Tessa's mittened hand carefully held in mine over the uneven terrain. "You doin' okay?"

"Uh-huh," she says, keeping up with my long strides,

her brown eyes sparkling from the exercise and cold. "I'm excited. I never cut down my own Christmas tree before."

"I had to get permission from the forestry service to cut one down just for you," Jim tells Gia.

"Wow," says Gia. "You must be important."

I roll my eyes. "Everyone in Craig gets permission! Hell, everyone in Alaska, practically! He's nothing special, Gia."

But Gia, who has a crush on Big Jim, rests her cheek on his knit hat-covered head and sighs, saying solemnly: "Yes, he is, Tony."

"If my daughter ends up marrying a big redheaded Irishman one day, I'll have Big Jim to blame," says Tessa, grinning at me.

"She could do worse than a guy like Jim," I tell her.

"Or she could hit the jackpot with a guy like you," she answers.

Jim and Gia are a ways ahead of us now, but I don't care. I pull Tessa into my arms, covering her always-warm lips with mine. When I lean away from her, I'm light-headed and breathless. I want more, as I always do. I can't get enough of this woman.

"I'm crazy about you," I say, searching her face to be sure it's okay I share these feelings with her.

Her eyes open slowly, and her lips tilt up in a sweet smile. "I feel the same."

"You do?"

"You aren't sure?" she asks, reaching up to cup my cheek with a colorful mitten. "I make love to you every night. I eat your breakfast and make your dinner. I'm safe.

I'm happy. You've made a home for me and my daughter." She leans up on tiptoes to brush her lips against mine again. "Yeah, I'm crazy about you, Tony. Of course I am."

***

Tessa

It's a lie, I think, *but a white one.*

I mean, I am *crazy about him—that's the truth—but it's just the tip of the iceberg.*

The iceberg is love.

I love him.

He kisses me again, and I meet his tongue stroke for stroke, pouring everything I feel, everything I want, into the movement of my lips, and the sighs of pleasure that he swallows. When he draws away and looks into my eyes, I think I see it there for a second, reflected in his expression: love.

"You make me happy," he whispers, nuzzling my nose with his.

"Same," I tell him, closing my eyes and savoring the moment.

"Tony!" yells Gia. "We found one!"

"Take your time," says Tony, who's carrying the ax. "Let's get started."

I watch him hurry ahead to join Jim and Gia, who dances around a massive pine tree with joyful abandon.

After three months in Alaska, I've really started to think of it as my home.

It's rural and small, yes, and far away from everything I

ever knew before, but I feel moderately safe here, and happier than I've ever been in my life. With my parents in Italy, I don't think I'll ever return to Jersey. In fact, if I get my way, Gia and I will stay in Craig, with Tony, forever.

That said, I don't live my life free of fear. Tony updates me occasionally about Santo's online posts—his ongoing search for me and Gia. But he tells me not to worry; that Santo will eventually give up looking for us just as he gave up looking for Tony.

I don't know if I believe him.

I *want* to believe him, but with Giancarlo gone, Santo has no child, no heir… except Gia. I can't imagine him ever giving up his quest for her. And even in this quiet, remote corner of the world, I don't feel completely hidden. I take my daughter to school, I go to work at the library, I come home to Tony every evening. But I'm always looking over my shoulder, and at least twice a week I wake up in a cold sweat, my nightmares about being found all too real. Tony holds me tight and rocks me back to sleep, but low-grade fear is my constant companion. Will it be like this for the next fourteen years?

Whack!

I look up to see Tony swing his ax again, his strong, broad shoulders rippling from the effort. *I love him. Dio mio, I love him so much.*

"Come on, Mamma!" calls Gia. "We're cutting down our Christmas tree!"

Shoving my worries aside, I smile at my baby, trudging through the deep snow to join my little family.

***

"So," I say, grinning at Rachel as I lift a mug of hot cocoa to my lips. "I can't stand it anymore! What's the deal with you and Jim?"

We're nestled on the couch together, warming up with some chocolate-y goodness while Jim, Tony, and Gia trim the tree. "What do you mean?"

"Rachel!"

"Okay. Okay," she says, rolling her eyes over the rim of her mug. "We're…you know…"

"Fucking?" I whisper.

"Tessa! No!"

Oh. I screw up my face in confusion. "Then, what are you—"

"We're… getting there."

"Kissing?" I ask.

Her cheeks instantly flush.

"You're kissing! You're making out!"

"Shhhh!" she hushes me, slapping my leg with her free hand. "Stop it."

"For the woman who leads the dirtiest book club in town, you're a total prude when it comes to talking about Big Jim," I grouse.

With my help, Rachel started Craig's Romance Addiction Book Club, the hottest Thursday night ticket on Prince of Wales Island. Fifteen of us get together in the library meeting room every week to talk about a different love story, and outside of my time spent with Tony and Gia, it's my favorite part of the week.

She laughs softly. "That's different. Those are just books. Jim is…"

"For real."

"Mm-hm," she sighs, grinning at Jim, who's lifting Gia so she can place an ornament on a high branch. "He's good to me, you know? He's been amazing since…"

"How's your dad doing?" I ask.

Her smile has faded. "Not great."

Rachel's father had a massive stroke in late November, which led to some brain damage and a quick decline in his health. He isn't expected to make it much past New Year's.

"Is the hospice nurse with him today?"

She nods. "She's been really great."

"He doesn't mind her being there?"

"I'm not sure he notices," she says softly. "He didn't even know who *I* was yesterday."

I place my mug on the coffee table and reach for my friend, gently pulling her into my arms. "I'm so sorry."

"Thanks, Tessa." She sniffles against my shoulder before pulling away. "How about *your* dad? How's he?"

"Knock on wood, he's been good since September."

"No more heart issues?"

I shake my head. "None that I know of. He and my mother seem happy. Italy's good for them."

"Any plans to go visit?"

While Jim knows the details of my history with the D'Angelos, Rachel doesn't. She thinks I answered Tony's personal ad and came to Alaska with the sole intent of meeting him; she has no idea that I actually came here to escape Gia's birth grandparents.

"Not for a while," I tell her. "It's far. And expensive. Maybe in a year or two."

"Thank God for email and the phone, huh?"

My smile feels forced. "Thank God."

The truth is, I miss my parents. I miss them something awful and waiting two more years to see them sounds like an eternity. But I have to believe that if Santo is searching for me and Gia in Alaska, he's also got people watching my parents. I won't put them—or Gia—in danger by risking a visit, even if that means I never get to see them again.

But the thought aches and tears spring to my eyes.

"Oh, Tessa!" says Rachel. "No! Don't cry."

I chuckle, swiping at my eyes. "We're a pair, huh?"

She nods, reaching for my hand and squeezing it. "At least we can be here for each other. I was lonely before you moved here."

"Me too," I say, and realize it's true.

I was surrounded by family in New Jersey, but somehow, I always felt left out and lonesome, especially after my parents moved to Italy. Being here with Tony has changed my life; has given new definition to "belonging."

Speaking of my love, he is suddenly standing in front of us.

"All done. Ready to see it?" he asks us. "Gia, turn off the overhead lights."

As my daughter races over to the light switch, he offers me his hand. I stand up, holding my breath as the room goes dark.

"Ready?" asks Jim. "One… two… three!"

The whole room lights up with the soft, magical glow of white Christmas lights. Rachel claps her hands in appreciation, Gia races to hug Jim, and Tony plants a sweet kiss on my forehead.

"Merry Christmas, Tessa," he whispers near my ear.

It's such a beautiful moment, and I feel so loved, a lump rises in my throat, making words impossible. I rest my head against Tony's chest, my heart overflowing with gratitude.

Merry Christmas, my love.

***

Hours later, when Jim has driven Rachel home and Gia is in bed for the night, I join Tony on the couch to admire the sparkling Christmas tree, our first together.

"Where'd you get all these lights and ornaments?" I ask him.

"I ordered 'em from Amazon after Thanksgiving," he tells me, putting his arm around my shoulders and pulling me closer, "when it looked like you and Gia would be staying through Christmas."

"Thanks for doing this for her," I say, leaning up to give him a quick kiss on the lips. "You're amazing."

He raises an eyebrow at me. "You call that a kiss, woman?"

"Oh," I murmur, "were you hoping for more?"

"Always," he says, chuckling wickedly as he puts his hands beneath my ass and lifts me onto his lap. "I can't get enough of you."

Straddling his waist, I let my knees dig into the couch as I face him. "The feeling's mutual."

"So, kiss me like you mean it," he commands, sliding his hands under my shirt to unclasp my bra.

Knock. Knock. Knock.

His hands freeze. He looks over at the front door, his eyebrows furrowing.

"Huh. Think Jim forgot something?"

I shrug, climbing off his lap. "Maybe."

Patting his ankle before standing up, he walks barefooted to the front door, unlocking the deadbolt—but not the chain—before opening it slowly.

I can't see who's on the doorstep, but my adrenaline rushes as Tony instantly tries to slam the door shut, struggling to push it closed.

"Run, Tessa!" he yells. "Get Gia and run!"

But frozen with fear, I can't move.

I watch in horror as an unseen force from outside snaps the chain in half.

The door crashes against the foyer wall.

Tony is hit in the face by the swinging door and falls backward onto the marble floor.

Shocked into action, I spring up from the couch, about to run upstairs, when two men surge into the house, one of them falling on Tony, while the other blocks my way to the stairs.

"Theresa Rinaldi," he says in a strong New Jersey accent, staring at me with a crooked smile. "Finally."

CHAPTER SIXTEEN

Tony

Tightly bound with rope to a kitchen chair, I can't do anything but struggle as Tessa shoots me terrified looks from the couch.

Patrizio "Pat the Cat" Catullo, looms over her, one hand on his revolver, the other holding his phone up to his ear.

"Yeah. Yeah, she's here." He pauses, looking at the ceiling. "Yeah. I checked. The kid's upstairs sleeping. You want that I wake her up?" He nods. "Got it, boss." He presses the End button on his phone, then pockets it, looking down at Tessa. "Santo's coming."

Her neck snaps up, her eyes red from crying. "S-Santo? He's here?"

I can hear the fear in her voice, and it kills me that I can't do anything to help her. I fight against the rope, but Joey "Whack" Lazio, one of Santo's strong arms, lays a beefy hand on my shoulder.

"Don't bother," he mutters. "You're not going anywhere. Don't waste your energy, Antonio."

"Antonio Silva," says Pat, looking over at me and

shaking his head. "Never thought we'd see *your* fucking face again."

"I thought Giancarlo did you when he did your uncle," says Joey.

"Fuck off, Joey," I growl, testing the rope at my ankles and finding it just as tight as the binding holding my chest and arms against the chair.

Joey backhands my face, splitting my lip open. "Always had a dirty fucking mouth on you."

"Where's Santo?" asks Tessa, her voice high-pitched and desperate.

"Landing in Klawock as we speak," says Pat, turning his attention back to her. "He's been waiting for news." He sits down in an easy chair across from her, training his gun on her kneecap. "He'll be here in half an hour."

She blinks away tears, her eyes shuttering open and closed quickly in panic.

"He's been staying up in Ketchikan for the last two weeks," Pat continues. "Since we started getting closer to youse."

Her shoulders crumple as she bows her head, and it's like I can read her mind: *While we were cutting down a Christmas tree, we should have been escaping.* How is it possible that she was straddling my lap not ten minutes ago? Our entire world's been shattered since then.

"Baby," I murmur, struggling to speak through my puffy lip. "It's… gonna be… okay."

Joey bashes the side of my head with his fist. "Yeah. It's all gonna be okay once Santo has his granddaughter safe and sound, and you're in the fucking ground."

I see stars for the third or fourth time since Pat and Joey arrived, but try to keep my head upright: they're going to take Tessa and Gina, and they're going to kill me. I've got to find a way out of this.

"Hey!" says Pat. "Sound and ground. You made a rhyme!"

Fucking imbeciles.

I need to think. I need to find a way out of this.

"How… how did you find me?" asks Tessa.

"Santo sent half his guys to Anchorage and Fairbanks and the other half rode the ferry lines outta Ketchikan. Once we got here, we asked about you at the local bar. Almost left too, since nobody ever seen a fat Italian chick and her kid around town… but then we lucked out. Saw you yesterday."

"*Saw* me?"

"Yeah," he says. "We saw youse walking from the library to the bus stop."

"You've been here for two days?" she asks.

Pat nods. "Yeah. We needed to be sure it was you. While you was out getting the tree today, we was here, looking around, making sure it was you. Woulda visited you sooner, but needed to wait 'til that big, redheaded motherfucker went home."

"Antonio," says Joey, cocking his head to the side. "How the fuck did you end up here?"

"Fuck… your mother," I mutter, spitting out a mouthful of blood on his shiny black shoes.

Joey hits me in the head again—harder than last time—

and pulls his gun, boring it into my temple. "I'ma kill this fucker, Pat."

"Stop it!" Tessa screams. "Don't!"

Pat laughs at her. "Honey, you know Joey's nickname?"

She shakes her head.

"*Whack Whack*. Wanna know why?"

Her eyes widen with fear. She licks her lips, and I can see her thinking.

"You don't want to wake up Gia! Santo said to let her sleep, right?" she asks him, wiping tears from her cheeks. "The gun. The bang… it would…"

He glances up at the ceiling with annoyance, then shrugs at Joey, who puts the gun back in its holster.

We sit in silence as Joey rummages through my refrigerator, opening a beer on the edge of my kitchen counter and nicking the marble in the process. Asshole.

Strangely, after three years of anticipating this day, I find I'm not that scared for me. I always knew my time could run out, and it's not like I lived a perfect life. Although I never killed anyone, I roughed up enough poor bastards at my uncle's request, I could see this final chapter as a sort of comeuppance. No matter how hard I tried to hide, it was always possible my past would eventually catch up with me and I'd have to pay the cosmic piper.

Any mobster knows this simple truth: a day of reckoning is always on the table. For life.

But Tessa and Gia? Fuck, I didn't want them to ever have to return to Jersey, let alone like this. Once Santo has them, he'll never let them go. They'll be dragged down to his level: mob pawns with targets on their backs, never able to hold their heads high or breathe freely again.

Tessa looks over her shoulder, her eyes finding mine, and my heart stutters from the fear and sadness I see there. *I wish I could've kept you safe*, I think. *I wish we'd had more time together, baby.*

The front door swings open and a blast of chilly air hits me in the face as Santo D'Angelo steps into my foyer with two of his associates flanking him. He's wearing a long, black winter coat, black leather gloves and some kind of a beaver hat. He looks fat and warm but seeing him sends an arctic chill down my spine.

"Antonio Silva," he says, pausing under the foyer chandelier for a second before looking at me. "Nice digs." He checks out the blood seeping from various wounds on my head, running slowly down my cheeks. "But you're not looking real good, son."

"Fuck you," I say, remembering the last time I saw him. *Fucking pop him, son, or I will.* "Piece of shit."

"Oh, no. Now, that's not polite," he tsks, nodding to Joey. "Take him out back and beat the shit outta him."

"You got it," says Joey, yanking at the rope behind my back.

"No!" screams Tessa, launching herself up from the couch and racing to Santo. She stands before him, wringing her hands. "Don't hurt him! I beg you!"

"You… *beg*… me?" asks Santo, pursing his lips. "You steal my only grandchild from me on the day of my only child's funeral and now you make demands of me? *Che palle*, eh, boys?"

His four henchmen mutter their agreement, waiting for their next command.

"What…" Tessa lifts her chin, staring up at Santo with so much fucking courage, it makes tears of pride prick my eyes. "What do you want?"

"Gia," he says, glancing at the staircase. His dead eyes level with Tessa's once again. "And because my sainted wife says a four-year-old needs her mother, you can come, too. If you behave yourself."

"Back to Newark," she whispers.

"Where else?"

"We could…" She gulps. "We could live here but promise to visit."

"Visit?" Santo says the word like it's a curse, then cracks a nasty smile. "That won't work for me. You'll come and live with me and Elena in our home: our daughter-in-law and beloved granddaughter, back where they belong."

"Daughter-in—but, Giancarlo and I weren't marri—"

"You don't say his name!" bellows Santo, shaking a stubby finger at her. "You don't *ever* say his fucking name!"

"I'll go with you…" Tessa glances at me again, then quickly back at Santo. "…if you promise to leave Tony alone."

"No!" I yell, tears falling down my cheeks. I know how men like Santo operate. Once he understands my worth to Tessa, he'll use it against her over and over again. If she tries to leave, tries to assert her independence, tries to make a decision he doesn't like, he'll threaten to kill me. It'll keep her in check. It'll make her his prisoner. She's trading her future for mine, and I can't fucking bear it. "No, Tessa!"

Joey takes a vase off of my kitchen counter and breaks it over my head, telling me to shut the fuck up. Shards of glass splinter and gather in my ear, and I struggle to stay conscious as more warm blood trickles into my eye, blinding me.

"Enough. I'll get the kid," Santo tells Pat, heading for the stairs. "Kill these two. Let's get going. Elena's waiting."

"She'll never forgive you!" cries Tessa as Santo's two bodyguards grab Tessa's arms, and Pat reaches for his gun. "Gia. She'll hate you! Forever! If you kill her mother, she'll never love you! She'll never love Elena! She'll never be your granddaughter in any way that matters! She's old enough to figure out what happened here! If she never sees me again, she'll know what you did. That you h-hurt me. That you killed me. She'll know. And she'll hate you."

Santo pauses, turning around and looking at Tessa with annoyance. He sniffs angrily, running a hand through his gray hair.

"You got balls. I'll give you that."

"I'm her m-mother," Tessa says through sobs. "Please… please don't…"

Santo nods, looking irritated. He points at me. "Okay. So, if I spare his worthless fucking life, you'll come willingly? You'll be nice about it? You'll make it easy for her?" His lip twitches. "For… for my Elena?"

"Yes. Yes. I p-promise!" The bodyguards ease their grip on Tessa as she nods frantically. "I'll go with you. I'll tell Gia we're having a fun adventure. I'll tell her how much her new nonna and nonni l-love her. I'll—I'll make it nice for Elena. I promise. She deserves to know her granddaughter. I promise I'll make it nice and easy." She gulps. "Just don't hurt him."

"Tessa," I groan, letting my head fall forward. "Don't... do this."

"I don't have a choice," she murmurs, tears cascading down her cheeks.

"Shut your mouth, Antonio, you piece of shit!" says Santo. He approaches me, drawing back his leather-gloved fist, then smashing it into my cheek. Bone shatters in my face. My vision clouds. The last thing I hear is this warning, low and close to my ear: "I ever catch you in Jersey, again, I'll slit her throat like a pig and bury her like a dog in the Pines. *Capiche?*"

With the last of my strength, I nod, then succumb to darkness.

CHAPTER SEVENTEEN

Tessa

♪ *"Jingle bells, j-jingle bells, jingle all - the wa-ay…"* ♫

Bing Crosby's cheerful croon, ably backed by the Andrews sisters' jaunty chorus, greets us at the front door of Elena and Santo D'Angelo's three million dollar Mediterranean-style mansion in Montclair, New Jersey.

We've been traveling since ten o'clock last night: a car to the Klawock Airport, a puddle jumper to Juneau, a short motel stay in a guarded room, and then a nine o'clock flight from Juneau that landed us in Newark a little after seven p.m.

Gia fell asleep in the limo from the airport, and I carry her sleeping body in my arms, despite offers from Santo's main bodyguard, Carmine, to carry her for me.

Elena D'Angelo stands in the center of an imposing marble foyer, under the glimmer of a crystal chandelier bearing a hundred lightbulbs and a holly garland. She is dressed in a light blue cocktail-length dress with her dark brown hair in a neat chignon. Pearls drip from her ears and cuff her wrists. In ivory-colored high heels and nude pantyhose, she looks every inch the society lady.

But when her eyes meet mine, I can see how fragile she is. Red-rimmed and bloodshot, hollow and dark. They tell me she hasn't stopped crying since the day she buried her son. Under her expensive costume, she's exhausted and empty, a shell of the elegant woman I'd seen at various community events since my childhood.

Except…

When her tired eyes slide from my face to Gia's, something miraculous happens; suddenly, she comes alive. Like there was a tiny ember hidden in the dark, lifeless depths of her eyes all along, I watch it catch and start to burn. It's small, yes, but it's there.

Life. Strength. Purpose.

My daughter makes her want to live.

"*Cara mia. Bambina mia*," she whispers, lifting her gaze to me. "She is so beautiful, Theresa."

"She's a piece of work," Santo tells his wife, stepping forward to kiss her cheek. "That's for sure."

"Does she look like…?"

"Yeah." Santo nods, his smile fading. "She looks just like him."

Elena nods, a terrible sadness reclaiming her visage, and dousing the flicker of life I'd just witnessed. She offers me a wan smile. "I'm so pleased you decided to come home."

Home? I stare at her, my compassion replaced by a fierce and instant fury. *Decided? Fat chance.* I silently marvel at the spin she's put on our veritable kidnapping, lifting my chin with indignance. If Elena notices this small act of defiance, it doesn't register on her face.

"You must be exhausted after traveling. May I show you to your rooms?"

A nudge in the small of my back reminds me of my promise to facilitate Gia and Elena's relationship. If I don't, Tony's life could be in the balance. As it is, we left him unconscious and tied to a chair, with broken bones and a probable concussion. He needs medical attention, and it chills me to the bone that I'm half a world away and can't help him.

"Theresa?" says Santo, the warning clear in his voice.

"*Grazie, signora,*" I whisper to Giancarlo's mother. "You're very kind."

"Oh!" says Elena. "I was hoping you'd call me '*Mamma*'. Santo told me that you and—and my son married in secret."

Interesting. So Gia's birth has suddenly been legitimized, like Giancarlo's renunciation of us never happened. What a crock of shit.

But Tony's battered face flashes before my eyes and tamps down my anger.

"Grazie… Mamma," I murmur, trying not to choke on the words or on Santo's revisionist history.

"Prego, tesora," she says gently, briefly cupping my cheek with a soft and manicured hand. Her eyes and tone appear to be genuine, which confuses me, because she's Santo's accomplice in all of this, isn't she? "I want us to be the very best of friends, Theresa. You have given us the greatest gift we could ever hope for. The only speck of light in a world of darkness."

I nod curtly, trying not to cry, then follow Elena up a grand marble staircase. As my weary legs climb, I look down at Gia, barely able to comprehend the hell I've consigned us to. We're D'Angelos now, whether we like it or not.

They give law-abiding, hardworking Italians a bad name.

My face flushes with shame as my father's words echo in my mind. How mortified my parents will be when I tell them we're living in Santo's house; when he insists that we take his name; when we're introduced around Newark as Theresa and Gia D'Angelo, Giancarlo's widow and daughter. *Dio mio*, how will I hold up my head?

"Here we are," says Elena, opening an ornate white door and leading us into a massive bedroom. She gestures to the satin-covered king-sized bed on one side of the room, and then to a fanciful twin-sized bed, covered with a beautiful, pink canopy, on the other side. "I thought you'd prefer being together… at least at first."

"Thank you," I say. "That was thoughtful."

"The bathroom is just over there." She smiles at me. "I want you to be happy here, Theresa. I want that more than anything."

Again, I have the disorienting feeling that she's being genuine with me: that she honestly believes I *chose* to bring my daughter back to this hell of a life.

"I'm sure… we will be," I mutter, half-choking on the lie.

Elena steps back toward me, planting a hand on my arm. "I don't know why my son kept you two a secret, but that's all in the past now. We're a family. We're together. As we should be."

A family.

I force myself not to wince as I remember cutting down our Christmas tree in Alaska yesterday, and musing on the fact that Tony, Gia, and I were building our own little family together.

"*Grazie*," I whisper.

"Get some rest, *tesora*," says Elena, leaning forward to rest her lips on Gia's forehead for a moment. "I'll see you both in the morning."

I'm motionless until I hear the door latch catch behind me, and then I cross the room and lay Gia on her brand-new princess bed. My vision blurry from tears, I feel my way around removing her coat and boots, then slide her little body under the covers. She frets for a moment before curling up in a ball and breathing deeply.

I unzip my coat, letting it fall to the floor as toe off my boots. I pause briefly at my satin-covered, sacrificial altar, where I've made *my* proverbial bed.

Scooting under the covers fully dressed, I cry myself to sleep.

***

Days melt into days until we've been living in Montclair for nearly a week, our pretty bedroom a self-imposed prison.

It's not that we can't move freely around the gigantic house and walled-in grounds, but there are guards who watch our every move, and explaining their presence and function to Gia has proved challenging. She's smart and observant, and—in her own words—our new home doesn't "feel right."

I couldn't agree more.

We don't see Santo very much (thank God), except at dinner, where we sit at a large, black, marble table where servants offer us a non-stop menu of Italian fare I can't seem to stomach. He's on his phone most of the time, leaving us to visit with Elena, who has become our one bright spot in Newark.

I don't want to like Elena—not initially, at least—but she is so gentle, so genuinely interested in making us comfortable in her home, it's hard not to become attached to her. I see that ember in her eyes flare up every so often; especially when Gia is being silly or misbehaving. I know that she's thinking of her son at a similar age, and part of me hopes that being around Gia is helping her grieve and helping her heal.

As for me, though, I feel like I'm falling apart.

This afternoon, I woke up from a nap to find myself alone in our room and raced into the hallway upstairs, panting with fear over Gia's whereabouts. Blindly following faint sounds of her giggles, I found her nestled beside Elena on the floor of the master bedroom, the two of them eating popcorn and watching "Rudolph, the Red-Nosed Reindeer" on a cinema-sized television.

"Gia!" I cried, panting with exertion and waggling an angry finger in my daughter's direction. "What the hell were you thinking? I couldn't find you! I was worried! You scared me!"

Elena had jumped up from the makeshift fort of

pillows, comforters, and blankets and placed a gentle arm around my shoulders.

"Shh, *tesora mia.*"

"She's *my* daughter, Elena! Not yours!"

Recoiling as if slapped, Elena let her arm slide from my shoulders, her body sagging. "We were—we were just building ice forts and watching Christmas movies." Wringing her hands together, she'd blinked against tears. "She's fine. See? She's fine, Theresa. I'd never hurt her. I'd die first."

As my heartbeat slowed down, I slid my eyes to Gia, whose giggles were long gone. She stared at me with confusion and fear, wondering why her momma was yelling and her grandmother was on the brink of tears. I caught a glimpse of my face in the mirror over Elena's vanity, horrified by my dark, drawn eyes, gaunt cheeks and wild hair.

Where was the happy woman who'd been forced to leave Alaska a week ago?

I'm coming apart at the seams.

Oh, Tony. How I miss you.

Swiping at a sudden well of tears, I shrugged away from Elena's touch and told them to enjoy their movie, trudging back to my room alone.

When we arrived, Elena had told me I was allowed to use the house phone in my room as much as I liked—to call my parents in Italy, get in touch with local family or contact friends. Although I emailed my parents to inform them of what had happened, I hadn't called anyone yet.

But now I lift the receiver and place it against my ear.

My tears fall freely as I imagine Tony's voice on the

line.

"Hello?"

"Tony? It's me!"

"Tessa!"

"I-I miss you. I miss you so much it aches."

"Aw, baby. I miss you, too…"

"I don't just miss you. I love you, Tony. I wish I'd told you to your face. I wish we'd had more time. I wish… I wish…"

I gulp over the painful lump in my throat as I place the receiver back in the cradle. What's the point of calling him? I'm trapped here with Gia for the next fourteen years, and Santo swore to kill Tony if he ever stepped foot in New Jersey again. We're star-crossed. We're impossible. Staying in touch will amount to nothing more than slow torture. A clean break is better.

Lying back on my bed, I stare at the ceiling, a deep, paralyzing and all-too-familiar depression sweeping over me as the door to my room clicks open.

"Tessa?"

At the sound of Elena's voice, I sit up. "Yes?"

She appears by my bedside, her dark eyes appraising. "Are you okay?"

No. No, I'm not. "Sure."

"Missing someone?" she asks, sitting down beside me. Her eyes, as usual, are kind. "Gia told me that you two were living with someone in Alaska. A man named Tony?"

Again, I'm disoriented by the feeling that Elena genuinely doesn't know the details of how I came to live with her. But she and Santo are married! They live together.

They share the same bed. How can it be possible that she doesn't know anything about his dealings? Does he purposely keep her in the dark? Or does she willingly live in a state of complacent complicity?

"Antonio Silva," I tell her, my voice wispy and broken. "From Bayonne. He moved up there a few years ago."

A spark. "Silva?"

I nod, sniffling tears away. "Yeah. Tony. He goes by Tony Silvestri now, but… yeah. When he lived here, his name was Antonio Silva."

"Angela's son," she whispers. "Marina's nephew."

Surprised she's so well-acquainted with Tony's family, I snap my neck to the right to see her face, her eyes. "Yes."

"We were friends," she murmurs, as though in a daydream. "Me and Angela and Marina. We went to St. Ann's together as girls."

"I had no idea."

"Oh, yes. We had such fun together…when the kids were little… before…" Her voice trails off as she stares wistfully into the distance at nothing.

How much do you know? I wonder. *Do you know your husband ordered your son to shoot Tony's uncle Gino? The husband of your childhood friend?*

"His uncle was shot three years ago," I say, watching her face. "Did you know that?"

With a sharp inhalation of breath, she clenches her eyes shut. Her jaw tightens, like she's grinding her teeth together. But after a moment, she lifts her chin, fixing that placid expression back on her face.

"I remember something about... an intruder," she whispers. "Poor man."

"An… *intruder?*"

…*named Giancarlo D'Angelo.*

"Mm-hm," she murmurs, patting my arm, then gripping it gently to steady herself as she stands up. She steps toward the door to leave, then surprises me by turning around. "There's no reason for you two to stay apart. You can go see Antonio whenever you want to, Theresa. You're not a prisoner here, and I'm happy to look after Gia while you're gone."

"I'll *never* leave her here alone," I vow, my voice teetering on the edge of hostile.

Pain flashes over Elena's face. "But she wouldn't be alone. She'd be with me."

"I'll *never* leave her," I repeat, more quietly, but no less firm.

Elena nods in resignation, even as tears flood her eyes. "I understand."

The door clicks closed behind her, leaving me alone.

***

After two weeks of seeing no one but Gia, Elena, Santo, and the D'Angelo's horde of bodyguards and servants, I wake up a week before Christmas desperate to get out of their house for a few hours. I need to get some presents for my daughter—no matter what's happened over the past few weeks, or how much it's broken my heart, I won't ruin Christmas for her.

With Gia now spending every afternoon from noon to

three at the most exclusive preschool in Montclair, I feel comfortable heading into Newark to go shopping. If I leave at twelve, I can be home when Carmine pulls back into the driveway at three-fifteen with Gia in the back seat.

Downtown, I swing into the Children's Place and Gap Factory Store, filling the trunk of Elena's BMW with shopping bags of clothes, stuffed animals, shoes, and toys. Then, realizing that I'm not far from my cousin's shop, I decide to stop for a quick hello before heading back to Montclair. Locking the car, I walk the two or three blocks over to Clinton Street, spying Francesca at the reception desk through the front window.

As I step through the door, her eyes widen.

"*Santa Maria*, look what the cat dragged in," she says, pursing her lips at me. "Long time, no see, cuz."

"Hey, Francesca," I say, pausing just inside the door, unable to tell if I'm welcome here or not.

"Bridget," she calls to a redheaded woman in her early twenties who's sweeping up around my old station. "I need to go out for a few. Answer the phone, yeah?"

"Sure," says Bridget, leaning the broom against the wall and taking Francesca's place at the desk.

"C'mon," says my cousin, shrugging into her coat and gesturing to the door. "Let's go get a coffee."

"Where we going?" I ask, falling into step beside her.

"They opened a Dunkin' up the block."

"We can't make coffee in the salon and talk?""

"No." She sighs, and it's a loud, long-suffering sound. "Things've changed, Tessa."

"How?"

She stops walking and gives me a dark look. "You *know* how."

I put my hand on her arm, keeping her from moving. "Say it."

"You're a D'Angelo now."

"No. I'm not."

"Yeah," she says, "you are."

Wrenching her arm away from me, she flings open the door of Dunkin' Donuts and heads for the counter, ordering two small coffees.

"You want anything else?" she asks me over her shoulder.

"No."

You're a D'Angelo now.

I cringe at her words.

The hell I am.

She joins me at a table near the window, pushing a paper cup of coffee toward me.

"I'm *not* a D'Angelo," I tell her.

"If you marry a D'Angelo," she says, like she's talking to a toddler, "then you're a D'Angelo."

"I didn't—I'm not *married* to a D'Angelo."

"You *were*," she says. "You know, Tessa, I didn't understand your reaction when I told everyone that Giancarlo was shot. I really didn't get it. I mean, fine, you two went to school together. Sure. But you got sick! All those tears for a boy you barely knew didn't track. Then I found out you two were married in secret? He's Gia's dad?

Jesus, Tessa!" She takes a sip of her drink. "Then I got it."

"I was *never* married to Giancarlo D'Angelo," I clarify. "Never ever."

"And he wasn't Gia's dad neither?" she asks.

I huff softly. "No. He is. He was."

She raises her eyebrows at me. "So?"

"I was his…"

"Fuck buddy?"

"Francesca!" I give her a scathing look.

"Just trying to understand," she says, pouring another packet of sugar into her coffee.

"You don't need to be a bitch about it."

"Do you know what it was like here?" she hisses, resting her elbows on the table and leaning closer to me. "All through September… October… November? With Santo and Vito's goons stopping by the salon… going to Mamma and Pappa's house… bothering the girls at work. Threatening us. Insisting we knew where you were. Why do you think your father had a heart attack? Jesus, Tessa! Am I a *bitch*? I guess I've earned the right to be!"

"I didn't know about all that," I say softly.

"Of course not. You skipped town and left us to deal with your mistakes!"

"Gia is not a mistake!" I cry.

"But getting involved with a D'Angelo was!" she bellows. Looking around the mostly empty café, she clears her throat and calms down. "I don't get it, Tessa. I don't understand. Your dad. My dad. They stayed strong. They never danced for the D'Angelos. They kept their noses clean.

Why did you do it? Why the hell would you hook up with Giancarlo?"

His face—Giancarlo's beautiful face—flashes through my head, and I'm reminded once again of how it felt for the hottest boy in Newark to want me. Me. Chubby, stubby, irrelevant Theresa Rinaldi. Every time he texted me, I went running. I couldn't help myself. Giancarlo became my world.

Suddenly, I think about the awful things I said to Tony during our first phone conversation, and for the first time since then, I see things through a different lens. Giancarlo used me, yes. But I wanted it. I *let* it happen. I let myself be used. It wasn't all his fault.

"I was weak," I confess. "He was…"

"Beautiful," says my cousin, nodding her head in understanding even as her lips remain pursed.

"Beautiful," I whisper.

We sit in silence for a few minutes, sipping our coffee, lost in our own memories of a man whom neither of us knew very well; who had an impact on both of our lives after he was gone.

"Bottom line is this: you're gonna bring trouble to me and mine if you come around. We don't want no part of your life with the D'Angelos," says Francesca. "You made your bed, Tessa. You gotta lie in it." She looks sad when she lifts her head to meet my eyes. "You're one of them now, whether you want to be or not."

"I'm not—"

She holds up her hands. "Yes, you are."

It's not like I expected to be invited over for the seven

fishes on Christmas Eve, but my cousin is essentially disowning me, and it's painful. My eyes fill with tears, blurring my vision.

"I'll always care about you," she says, pushing away from the table and standing up. "But you're a D'Angelo, hon. That's all there is to it."

She throws away her empty coffee cup and I watch through the window as she walks briskly back down the street to her salon.

Never, in my entire life, have I ever felt lonelier…

…which leads me to make a very stupid decision.

CHAPTER EIGHTEEN

Tony

When my cell phone rings with an unfamiliar number, I stare at it for a second, trying to tamp down the rush of hope I feel.

"Hello?"

"T-Tony?"

Her voice.

Just the sound of her voice makes my heart swell and pound.

"Tessa!"

She sniffles. "Y-Yeah. It's me."

Her tears frighten me. "You okay, baby?"

"Y-Yeah.," she manages, her voice broken and soft. "I'm just—it's so g-good to hear your voice."

She's sobbing now, but as long as she's not in danger, I can bear it. I rub my eyes, which are suddenly burning.

"They treating you okay?"

She takes a jagged breath and sighs into the phone. "Y-Yeah."

She's upset and I can't help her, can't hold her, can't reassure her. It kills me. I cradle the phone between my ear and shoulder, fisting my hands together and wishing I could punch something.

"Talk to me. Tell me what's going on."

She sniffles again. "My cousin—Fran-ch-ch-cesca—she said I'm a… D'Angelo."

"No, you're not," I tell her firmly. "You had no choice. God help me, baby, but you had no choice. You had to go with them."

"I know," she murmurs, sadness weighing down her voice. "I wish we could have stayed with you, Tony."

"Me too."

"How're *you*?" she asks in a rush. "Last time I saw you—"

"Fine!" I assure her. "Believe it or not, that wasn't the worst beating I ever got. Jim stopped by the next day when I didn't pick up an order of lumber at the yard. Untied me. Got me to urgent care. No big deal. Good as new, now."

I'm lying to her. In addition to several broken ribs, my liver was bruised, my cheekbone was fractured, my nose was broken, and I had a concussion. But telling her this won't help anything. I don't want her worrying about me, especially now, when I'm almost back to normal.

"That guy—he broke glass over your head."

"Like I said, not my worst beating," I tell her. "Anyway, I'm all cleaned up now. Don't worry about me. Tell me about you. And Gia."

"Gia's good," she says, her voice brightening a fraction. "She's going to this fancy preschool in Montclair. Elena chose it."

Elena, huh?

Hearing my girl refer to Elena D'Angelo in such cozy and familiar terms sends a chill down my spine.

"She likes it?"

"She liked the one in Craig better."

This soothes me a little.

"She likes her, uh, grandparents?"

"She's frightened of Santo and his guys," she tells me, "but she and Elena have gotten close."

Elena, again.

I purse my lips.

"How about *you* and… *Elena*?"

"She's kind to me," she says quietly.

Inroads, I think. *To get to the kid, you've got to get to the mother.* It's the oldest trick in the book, and Elena D'Angelo, with her pretty clothes and soft voice, has always been an asset to Santo in this department. The yin to his yang in personnel matters, she's the softness that balances out his cruelty.

I despise her.

"She knew your mother," says Tessa, making bile rise in my throat. "And your aunt. They—"

"—went to the Convent of St. Ann's together," I finish, remembering a picture my aunt once showed me: of herself, with my mother and Elena D'Angelo in their school uniforms at the annual Feast of the Assumption fair. I open the door to my back deck and sneer at the snowy landscape. "Long before her husband put out a hit on my uncle."

"Sometimes…"

She doesn't finish her thought.

"What?"

"Sometimes I wonder if she knows."

"About what?"

"Santo. The mob. Everything."

"She buys her clothes at Nordstrom's because the sanitation business is so lucrative?" I ask sarcastically. "She's not an idiot, Tessa."

"Obviously she knows that Santo has alternate income streams," says Tessa.

"Obviously," I say, crossing my arms over my chest.

"But does she know *all* of it? About *everything*?"

"Like what? Murder? Kidnapping? Extortion? Torture?"

"Yeah. Sometimes I get the feeling she doesn't know."

"She knows," I tell Tessa.

"But—"

"She may not know where all the bodies are buried, but she knows she's married to a mobster. And she doesn't get in his way." I pause for a second before my true thoughts come tumbling out. "I *hate* her. I hate her almost more than him because she profits off the misery of others. She doesn't get her hands dirty. She just enjoys the benefits."

This admission is greeted with a couple of seconds of dead air, and I can feel Tessa's conflict through the miles between us. She wants to like Elena. And fuck. Maybe her survival depends on it. I'm a selfish fucker to take it away from her.

"You do you," I tell her, trying to soften my tone.

"Between a grizzly and a wolf, there are no good choices."

"If anything," she says, "Elena's a wolf… with her foot caught in a trap. How's she supposed to—"

"I get it that you have to like her or she's nice to Gia or something," I tell Tessa. "But I can't—I mean… can we change the subject? Please?"

"Of course," she says. "How… um… how's Big Jim doing?"

"Fine."

"Things still progressing with Rachel?"

I don't tell her that I haven't hung out with them since she left. It hurts too much to see them happy when I'm missing Tessa and Gia with every fiber of my being.

"They look happy." I take a deep breath. "Her dad doesn't have long, though."

"Oh, no," she says. "Tell her I'm thinking about her? I'm sorry I can't… be there."

"Yeah." *Me too.*

More silence, and it's heavy with unspoken feelings and untold longing. It's deep and painful—almost too much to bear. I know she must feel it too.

"I want to get back to Montclair before Gia gets home at three," she says softly. "I don't like her to be alone with them."

"Don't go yet!" I blurt out, my chest tightening at the thought of losing this connection to her.

"Tony, I—"

"Nobody ever did anything for me like you did!" I cry. "Putting me before yourself. You saved my life. He woulda… he woulda killed me for sure, Tessa. You saved me. You saved me, baby." She doesn't say anything, and my brain recognizes this as permission to keep talking. "You put me before anything, and since my parents died, no one's ever… I mean…" Tears roll from my eyes and I'm glad she can see them. "It's not over. *We're* not over."

"Tony," she says softly.

"We'll figure this out. If it's the last thing—"

"It *will* be the last thing," she says, reminding me of Santo's promise to kill me if I ever step foot in New Jersey again. "You can't do anything. He'll kill you if you come to me, and I'll never leave my baby with them."

"Tessa—"

"Forget about me."

"Never."

"Let me go," she says, an edge of desperation in her voice. "At least for now."

"Baby, please—"

"Just—just remember we were happy."

"Tessa—"

"Remember that you…" She pauses for a second, then finishes: "You were loved, Tony."

I suck in a sharp breath as her words hit their mark, exploding my heart and rendering me mute.

"I couldn't let them hurt you because I love you," she whispers.

Tell her you love her, too. Say something. Say anything!

"I have to go, Tony," she says. "Goodbye."

The phone goes dead.

"Tessa? Tessa!" I yell, regaining my wits. "Tessa! Come back! Tessa!"

But she's gone.

She's long gone, and I didn't get a chance to tell her that I love her, too.

***

Now that the D'Angelos know my whereabouts, and I have the freedom to travel anywhere in the world except New Jersey, I spend my first Christmas in three years with my Zia Marina and cousins in Florida.

I appreciate not having to hide anymore, but since my love has moved back to Jersey, I can't seem to find peace or happiness anywhere—even with my family. As intuitive as ever, and having raised me from a boy, my aunt notices the changes in me right away. The day after Christmas, while my cousins and their kids are splashing around in the pool, my aunt takes a seat next to me.

"Sun's strong today," she says, settling into a lounger and adjusting the brim of her hat to keep the sun off her face.

"Isn't it strong every day?"

"No. Sometimes it rains," she says, nudging my knee. "You've changed."

"Subtle, as always, Zia."

She chuckles, staring at her grandchildren in the pool.

"Why beat around the bush?" she asks rhetorically. "It's just a waste of time."

"What do you want to know?" I ask her.

"Her name."

I don't bother lying. There's no point.

"Theresa."

"Theresa… what?"

"Rinaldi."

"From Bayonne?" she asks.

"Newark."

"Rinaldi the plumber or Rinaldi the brick mason?"

"Plumber," I tell her, perpetually amazed by my aunt's effortless recall. It feels like she knows—or knew—every family in northern New Jersey at one point or another.

She nods. "Napolitanos. Kept to themselves."

"That's them."

Tessa had shared with me her father's disdain for families like the D'Angelos. Her father said that Italian-American families who bent the knee to the local mob gave honest, hard-working families a bad name.

"Didn't know them except by reputation."

"Tessa had a daughter with Giancarlo D'Angelo," I tell her. "*Has* a daughter. She's four."

"I see." Her voice is brittle and cool. She knows as well as I do that Giancarlo killed her husband. "I'm surprised at you, Antonio, associating with—"

"She's no friend of the D'Angelos, Zia. In fact, he never acknowledged her or the kid," I tell her. "Tessa left Newark when Santo figured out that Gia was his granddaughter."

"Ah."

I tell her about Tessa's escape to Alaska, about how she showed up on my doorstep claiming to be my cousin. I tell her how I somehow fell in love with this short, pudgy woman, who wasn't even a little bit my "type."

"Type. Ha. *Bambino*!" says my aunt with a sniff. "Into your twenties, you were still a silly little boy. Maybe because you lost your parents early, God bless them. Or maybe you just got turned around at some point. But you dated a parade of stupid, beautiful women. No substance. No heart. No… nothing."

"Thanks, Zia," I deadpan.

"Hey, I'm giving you a compliment," she tells me. "Wait for it!"

"I'm waiting…"

"You were a cocky boy. A selfish little boy playing with women like toys. Now? You're a man. You're sick and you're frustrated and you're tired and you're hurting. It brings my heart joy, Antonio! You're a man. A good man. Like my brother. Your father, bless his soul."

My heart squeezes. It's the best compliment I've ever been given.

"You think so?"

"Yes," she says, with conviction, without embellishment.

I bask in her words as the sun beats down on us.

"She loves you, this Theresa."

A statement, not a question, but I answer it anyway. "God knows why."

"Because you're a good man, Antonio. Kind. Protective. Funny. Handsome as sin."

I push my sunglasses down a little and wink at her.

"Keep your winks," she says, pushing me away. "You love her, too."

"More than I ever knew possible."

"Okay, then." She shrugs. "So… you wait."

"I…*wait?*"

"How old is the child? Giancarlo's daughter?"

"Four."

"So… you wait fourteen years. Big deal." She snaps her fingers. "It'll fly."

I remember Tessa's warm, soft, naked body burrowed into mine and sigh. "It *won't* fly."

"Love like this? It's once in a lifetime," she says, patting my leg. "You wait."

A moment later, she jumps up, shucks off her cover-up and jumps into the pool with her grandchildren, splashing around like a teenager. I grin at her antics, and for the first time in weeks, I realize I'm not angry. I'm frustrated, sure. And I'm missing Tessa like crazy. But I feel something suspiciously like hope, and it doesn't feel bad.

You wait.

I can do this, I tell myself.

For as long as it takes.

You wait.

CHAPTER NINETEEN

Tessa

"Mam-m-m-m-a," whines Gia, dressed to the nines in a red velvet dress with white fur at the neck and cuffs. The black patent leather shoes on her feet gleam, and her white tights are practically blinding. She loves the outfit Elena purchased for her and has been counting down the days to New Year's Eve so she could wear it. "I wanna go down to the party."

"No, baby," I tell her, ignoring the sound of the jazz band downstairs. "We'll stay up here tonight."

"Why?"

Because God only knows who's down there.

"I'm the mom," I remind her, smoothing the skirt of my black cocktail dress. I refuse to wear anything more festive. "I make the decisions and you follow them."

"You're just being mean!"

"I wish it was that simple, *bambina mia*."

She stamps her foot. "Nonna said there's cupcakes! And a mini fireplace to roast marshmallows. And a chocolate fountain!"

"I'll go down in a little bit and make a plate for you," I tell her.

"I don't want a *plate*! I wanna see it all!"

An unfortunate side effect of us living with the D'Angelos over the last four weeks is that Gia's been spoiled rotten. Christmas was an embarrassment of riches, of course, but I'm talking about *every day*. If Gia indicates the slightest interest in something—a type of food, a toy she sees on TV, an electronic gadget owned by one of her friends at school—Elena sends out one of Santo's guys to buy it for her. It's endeared Elena to Gia on a superficial level, but I don't like it one bit. I don't think it's healthy. Not to mention, my once well-behaved child has started throwing these little tantrums when she doesn't instantly get her way.

"You use that tone with me again," I tell her, "and you'll get nothing. *Capiche*?"

"Yeah. Fine!" Tears fill her eyes. "But maybe I hate you a little, Mamma."

She's never said anything like this to me, and it cuts me to the quick, but I lift my chin, shrugging like her words don't hurt me.

"Maybe you hate me *a lot*," I say. "But I'm your mother, not your friend. Hate me all you want. I'll still do what's best for you."

"I *don't* hate you!" she wails. "I *love* you!"

She throws herself onto my lap, and I cuddle her against me, stroking her curly hair as she sobs.

"I love you, too," I tell her. "But that was a very mean thing to say to Mamma."

"I j-just wanna go to the p-a-a-a-arty," she manages through tears.

"I know," I tell her. "I'm sorry you can't go."

"I'm sorry I said I hate you. I could *never* hate you, Mamma."

When the door to our room is thrown open, I jump. I know we live in Santo and Elena's house, but they've been respectful, thus far, knocking before entering and announcing themselves when they stand in the doorway.

Not tonight.

Santo enters the room red-faced and sweaty and stalks to the side of my bed.

"Why aren't cha downstairs?" he demands, towering over us in a black tuxedo that makes him look like an angry penguin. His breath smells of liquor and there's a lipstick stain on his collar. "People are waiting to see you. And *her*."

"We don't feel well," I mutter.

"You look fine!" he bellows.

Gia looks up at Santo, and I note, as I have before, that her little muscles clench as she gazes at him. She's frightened of him—she has been since the day he tore her from her bed in Alaska and took us, both weeping, from Tony's home. She sits up, leaning into me, her bottom lip quivering.

"Why's the kid upset?" he shouts.

"You're yelling," I say. "You're frightening her."

"Fuck that! Elena got all sorts of shit for the kid. Chocolate fountains and all sorts of shit! Cost me an arm and a leg. Get your asses downstairs—" He gives me a meaningful look. "Or I make a move on Mr. Alaska."

"Mr. Alaska? Tony's from Alaska!" exclaims Gia, scanning her grandfather's face with hope. "Is Tony here? Is he downstairs? Is *he* Mr. Alaska?"

Santo slides his eyes to her, his expression harsh. "Tony's lucky he's not dead, what with the way your mother's behaving."

"*Dead*?" asks Gia, misunderstanding him. Her eyes widen. "Tony's *dead*?"

"No!" I say. "No, baby. Tony's not dead. He's fine. He's up in Alaska living in his house. He's fine, honey. I promise."

"He'll *be* fine," says Santo, "as long as you and your mother behave yourselves. If not…"

He draws a finger across his throat.

"Don't do that!" I cry, springing to my feet. "Don't you *dare* threaten him! Or her!"

"Whoa. Wait a second, now." Santo's eyes narrow to slits. "Are *you* giving *me* a fucking order?"

I'm scared by the look in his eyes, but I don't back down. I try to lower my voice a touch, though, so as not to escalate the situation. *Think of Gia. Think of Gia.*

"I-I'm telling you that you're frightening her," I say, taking a step back. "And I don't like you threatening her."

I ever catch you in Jersey, again, I'll slit her throat like a pig and bury her like a dog in the Pines.

His threat to Tony pings in my head and my heart rate speeds up. He wouldn't actually do that, would he?

"Please," I add, trying to be polite.

"Please," he repeats, mimicking me.

His lips twitch, tilting up. It's a mean expression. A cruel and creative expression. He was pissed when he walked into this room; now he's furious, and this look tells me he's going to exact some revenge.

"Beg," he says.

"What?"

"Get on your knees and fucking beg me for what you want."

I suck in a sharp breath, staring at him, dumbfounded.

"Do it," he growls.

"You—you want me to beg for you not to frighten and threaten your granddaughter?"

"I want you to remember your *fucking place*," he says, putting a hand on my shoulder and pushing downward. His voice lowers to a dirty sneer. "Now, get on your knees… and beg. Like a fucking dog."

"Mamma," says Gia from behind me. "What's happening?"

"Nothing, honey," I tell her, resisting the pressure of Santo's hand. "Nonni's just—"

"Your mother keeps forgetting that she's my *fucking guest*!" Santo bellows. "She's going to kneel down in front of me and beg for my forgiveness, and then you and your mother are going downstairs to—"

"FUCK! YOU!" I scream, finally at the end of my rope. "Fuck you, Santo D'Angelo! You give decent Italian-Americans a bad name! GO FUCK YOURSELF!"

My father's words, that I'd heard all my life, fly out of my mouth before I can stop them. I stare at Santo in horror as he lifts the hand on my shoulder, draws it back, and slaps my face so hard I fall backward. Knocking Gia to the floor with my fall, I slump against the side of the bed, stars exploding behind my eyes as my cheek and jaw erupt into a white-hot burn from the fury of his smack.

I sputter in shock and pain as Gia screams, "Mamma!" from beside me.

"G-Gia," I mutter, trying to open my eyes all the way and blinking at the sharpness of the pain in my face. I reach in her direction, wanting to comfort her. "Gia. Come here. I-I'm…"

"Now," says Santo, his voice eerily calm as he stands over us. "*Beg.*"

I feel my daughter move beside me. She jumps to her feet and stands in front of me, her fur-cuffed hands on her tiny hips as she places herself between me and her grandfather.

"Don't you t-touch her again!" Gia screams through sobs. "Don't you ever hit my mamma again!"

"What's going on in here?"

Elena's voice overlaps Gia's cries, and when my eyes focus, I see her standing behind Santo in an elegant red velvet dress, her eyes darting from me to Gia and back to me.

"Tessa? *Tesora?* Are you—"

"She's fine," says Santo, glancing at Elena over his shoulder. "She slipped and fell."

"She didn't slip!" Gia yells. "He *hit* her! Nonni *hit* my mamma! I *hate* him, Nonna! I *hate* him!"

"*Bambina mia*!" cries Elena, crossing in front of her husband to squat in front of Gia. "Don't say that, my little love!"

Gia flings herself against her grandmother, weeping. "He… h-hit… m-my… m-mamma. Help her, Nonna. Help."

"Santo," says Elena softly, lifting her eyes to her husband. "We have guests downstairs. Please go visit with them, darling."

Santo stares at her for a moment, his once-angry face morphing into tenderness as he gazes down at his wife.

"Yeah," he says, running a hand through his salt and pepper hair. He pats Elena on the shoulder gently and nods. "Yeah. Okay. I'll do that."

Without another word, Santo leaves us alone, closing the door behind him.

Elena holds on to Gia with one hand and reaches for my injured cheek with the other. I flinch, pulling away from her.

"*Theresa mia.* Please. Let me help you."

I stare into her beautiful eyes, carefully made-up for the party downstairs.

"He hit me," I tell her.

She takes a deep breath and sighs softly. "You fell."

"Elena," I say, hot tears trailing down my cheeks. *When did I start crying?* "He *hit* me. Look at my cheek. He—"

"Shhh.," she hushes me. "Let's not speak about it."

"He *hit* me," I half sob, half scream, desperate to be heard and validated by this woman. "You can *see* it. You *know* it's true."

"Gia," says Elena, gently pushing her granddaughter off

her lap, "be Nonna's helper and get Mamma a cold washcloth from the bathroom? There's a good girl."

"Elena," I whisper.

"We'll cool down that cheek and get some make-up on it," she says, looking at my face, but making no move to touch me again. "No one will be able to tell."

"She hates him," I whisper. "She's terrified of him. Gia's terrified of Santo."

Elena's eyes meet mine.

"This will *never* be her home," I say, reaching up to gently swipe at my wet cheeks, one of them far more painful and swollen than the other. "*Please* let us go."

"Back to Antonio Silva?" she asks.

I nod. "Please. I beg you. If not for me, for Gia. She can't grow up here like this. Please, Elena. Please."

Gia races back to us, slowly and carefully handing me the cold, wet, dripping washcloth. "Nonna said to get this for you."

I take it from her and press it against my cheek. Droplets of water fall onto my dress, making it splotchy.

"Thank you, baby," I say, but I'm still staring at Elena and my eyes are begging her to help us.

She stares back at me, stone-faced. But it occurs to me that she's not denying Santo's behavior, and she's not saying "no" to me.

"How many more people you love have to die?" I whisper urgently. "Wouldn't you rather your granddaughter was safe? Wouldn't you rather she grow up happy?"

Elena mewls softly, but it's the only indication that

she's heard me. Her eyes search mine, and it's an intense, profoundly personal mother-to-mother moment, though I have no idea the effect I'm having on her.

Finally, she gulps softly and stands up.

"Clean yourselves up," she tells us, offering a tight, small smile that doesn't reach her eyes, "and come downstairs."

She didn't hear me, I think, watching her leave the room.

We're trapped here.

And there's no one who can help us.

With the cold washcloth still pressed against my cheek and my daughter sitting silently by my side, I bite the sides of my cheeks to stop crying, not stopping when I taste the metallic heat of my own blood.

***

Tony

I finally agree to go out to dinner with Jim and Rachel, mostly because Jim won't stop asking and his constant invitations are driving me up a fucking wall. I check out my haggard reflection in the foyer mirror before grabbing my keys and heading outside to my truck.

It's a dark, quiet ride into town and gives me too much time to think.

It's been almost a month since I heard from Tessa, and two weeks since I returned from Florida. I'm no less determined to "wait" for her, but I confess that the prospect of waiting was a lot easier when I wasn't in the place where Tessa, Gia, and I shared so many happy memories.

When I arrived home from Florida, I half expected to see Gia in the front foyer, greeting me with one of her famous wrap-around-my-leg hugs. I imagine finding Tessa in the kitchen making lasagna, or wistfully remember the three of us snuggled together on the couch watching a movie. I reach for Tessa in that hazy moonlight of early morning when the skies are still dark and my hands tremble with longing, desperate to feel the warmth of her skin beside me. It's torture. And right now, at least, I can't imagine a day when it'll get better.

I park near the entrance of Papa's Pizza and pull up my hood as I leave the car. I can see Jim and Rachel at a table by the windows, and I pause for a second, checking out the way they're looking at each other across the small table, their hands clasped over a red and white checkered tablecloth.

Rachel leans forward to say something and Jim's eyes widen for a second before he throws back his head and chuckles with delight. Rachel's lips tilt up as Jim laughs, her face filled with happiness.

My stomach clenches with jealousy and I look down at my scuffed boots in a puddle of muddy-brown snow-water.

I don't want to go to dinner with them.

I wish I was anywhere else but here.

Even New Jersey.

Pulling my phone out of my back pocket, I type *Alaska Airlines* into my browser and bring up the flight schedule for Newark, marveling that if I left now, I could be with Tessa in a matter of hours.

"Yeah," I mutter. "I mean, you'd be dead, sure. But at

least you'd be closer."

I shove the phone back in my pocket, gulping with misery.

It's only been fourteen days since I heard her voice. How the fuck am I supposed to make it fourteen *years*?

My phone buzzes against my ass, and I pull it back out, wondering if I called Alaska Airlines by mistake, and I'm surprised to see a phone number with a New Jersey area code pop up on my screen.

"Tessa?" I ask in a rush.

"No."

My blood runs cold.

"Who is this?" I ask.

"Am I speaking to Antonio Silva?"

"Yeah," I answer breathlessly. "Who the fuck is this? Is Tessa okay?"

"Theresa is fine," she answers. "My name is Elena D'Angelo. I assume you know who I am."

Every muscle in my body tenses. And my nostrils flare. Like, I *feel* them flare, and a moment later, when I exhale, my breath creates a puff of smoke that takes a second to disperse into the cold Alaskan skies.

I'd rip you limb from limb if I could, lady.

"Yeah," I say through gritted teeth. "I know who you are."

"Good."

"Whaddaya want?"

"To talk to you."

"About what?" *Perhaps the way your shit heel of a husband*

ordered your fucking son to kill my uncle?

"Theresa and Gia."

My heart skips a beat. "What about them? Are they okay?"

"I already told you… Theresa is fine."

"What about Gia?"

"She's…" Her voice catches. "She's fine, too."

"Thank God," I murmur. "You wanna talk about Theresa and Gia?"

"Yes, I do."

"Well, your fucking husband said he'd butcher me if I showed up in New Jersey, so I can't imagine what this call is regarding, Missus D'Angelo. Why don't you cut to the fucking chase, huh?"

She chuckles softly. "You remind me of your mother."

I don't want to be affected by these words, but I am, so I remain silent, letting the words "you remind me of your mother" pour over me like warm water on this freezing night.

"Angela was always a straight-shooter," she continues. "No time for bullshit."

"Elena D'Angelo cursing," I comment, remembering her as a "my-shit-don't-stink" style lady. "Is there a new world order?"

This time when she laughs, it's a soft, sad sound. "I should have spent more of my life cursing."

"You still have time," I tell her.

She changes the subject. "I'm sorry for what happened to your parents."

"Thanks."

"And… your uncle."

I can't thank her for her sympathy this time. My parents died in an accident. My uncle was murdered in cold blood by her son. I'm silent, and she finally speaks again:

"How's your Zia Marina doing?"

"Leave her alone," I growl.

"I would never—she was my friend," says Elena earnestly, and I remember Tessa questioning Elena's involvement in or knowledge of Santo's shady dealings. She *does* sound sincere, and it's confusing. "I'd never hurt her, Antonio. Is she well?"

"She's fine," I mutter.

"That's good to hear. Give her my best, won't you?"

I've had enough. "What do you want, Missus D'Angelo?"

"Since we've been chatting, you asked about Theresa twice and Gia once."

"Yeah. So?"

"You care for them. I mean, I think you do."

I take a deep breath. "Yeah."

"You *love* them?"

"Yeah." I clear my throat. "Not that it's any of your fucking business."

"Maybe it is," she says.

"What does that mean?"

"It means that I think Theresa and Gia were happy with you." She pauses. "Am I wrong about that?"

"We were happy together," I whisper.

"My… my son…" I hear her gulp softly on the other

side of the line. "I don't think my son treated them very well."

"He treated them like shit," I tell her.

She gasps softly and I feel the slightest bit of satisfaction mixed—surprisingly—with a little bit of regret. No matter what he did, he was her son, after all, and my words just hurt her.

"Yes. Well." She gulps again. "How would *you* treat them? If… if they were there, back in Alaska, with you?"

"Same way I treated them when they were here," I say. "Good."

"For how long?"

I glance up at Rachel, who knocks on the window, beckoning me into the pizzeria. I hold up a finger.

"What does that mean?" I ask her.

"Would they be safe with you?" she presses me.

"Of course."

"For how long?"

"What are you asking me?" I demand, feeling frustrated.

"You only knew them for a few months," she says, an edge of desperation coloring her tone. "Are you in this for the long haul? Or were they just… convenient?"

"You think they're *convenient*?" I scoff. "They arrived on my doorstep without a penny, claiming to be my family. I didn't know 'em from Adam. But they… I mean…" I find myself smiling as I remember picking them up on the side of the road; Tessa in those ridiculous fucking shoes, and Gia hitching a ride on the back of her mother's rolling suitcase.

"I fell for them. For *both* of them. For me, they were a little bit of home in the middle of nowhere. And… I guess I was the same for them. A sanctuary, you know? A safe harbor. Tessa, with her sassy fucking mouth, and Gia with her hugs every day when I got home from work. I just…" I clench my teeth together. "I want them back. I want them fucking back, Elena."

"I know," she murmurs. "I know you do."

"And to answer your fucking question… yes, I'm in it for the long haul. I mean, Jesus, I already decided to wait for Tessa. No matter how long it takes."

"You did?"

"I'm not gonna meet another like her."

"And you'll love Gia?" she asks, her voice tentative and serious at the same time. "Despite…"

Despite the fact that your kid killed my uncle?

"Yeah," I tell her. "I'll love her. I *do* love her. Despite *everything*."

She sniffles softly. "Promise me, Antonio. You'll treat them right. You'll be good to them. *Forever*."

"I promise," I whisper. Then I beg, too, because a plea rises up from my desperate soul: "Give them back. Please."

"I have to go," she says, her voice breaking.

"No. Elena, tell me how—"

"Take care of yourself, Antonio," she says. "Remember your promises."

"Wait! Elena, you have to tell me…"

I pull the phone from my ear and stare at the screen, but the call is gone, and the line is dead. I hit redial twice, but the callback goes nowhere.

She used a burner.

Why did Elena D'Angelo just call me with a fucking burner?

What the fuck is going on?

I stare at my phone for a couple of minutes, then shove it back in my pocket, my cheeks finally registering the cold. I rub them with my gloves, reminding myself that she said Tessa and Gia were safe, and praying that she was telling the truth.

Rachel knocks on the window again, and with a hundred more questions than answers, I trudge into the restaurant to join my friends.

CHAPTER TWENTY

Tessa

"Carmine," says Elena from the back of the limousine, where she sits beside Santo, and across from me and Gia. "You don't need to come inside tonight. We've been going to La Scala since before we were married."

"Carmine's coming," Santo grunts. "You never know—"

"I'm asking for a dinner alone with my family," Elena says gently, leaning her head closer to Santo's so Carmine, who's sitting in the front passenger seat, can't hear her. "Without your bodyguard looming over the table like a sentry." She takes Santo's hand and squeezes it. "That's all I want for my anniversary."

"Too bad," says Santo, gazing at her with love in his eyes. It's a tender look reserved only for his wife. "I got you other stuff, too." He shrugs. "Fine. Carmine, stay in the car with Giorgio tonight. If I need you, I'll call."

"You got it, Mr. D," says Carmine from the front seat before sliding the privacy window shut.

"I don't like going nowhere without him," says Santo, patting at his jacket nervously. The bulge over his heart tells me we're not going to dinner unarmed, even if Carmine stays in the parking lot.

Tonight is Elena and Santo's thirty-fifth anniversary, and the original celebration, planned over a year ago, was supposed to include their son, in addition to two hundred other friends and family. Instead, it's been paired down to the four of us at a local restaurant favored by Elena.

She's dressed in a black cocktail dress adorned with onyx crystals while Santo wears a "tough guy" power suit. Gia wears the emerald-green taffeta party dress Elena chose for her, and I'm wearing the same black cocktail dress I wore on New Year's Eve. Whatever blood from my lip and nose splattered onto the satin fibers have since been cleaned by one of Elena's many servants.

Not that I care.

I don't care about much lately.

After what happened on New Year's Eve, I've kept to myself, rarely leaving my room, and avoiding Santo at all costs.

I don't talk to my parents or local family in Newark; they've all but disowned me, and the shame I feel at living with the D'Angelos paralyzes me when I consider reaching out to any of them.

On one hand, I guess it could be said that I'm accepting my lot and coming to terms with this life.

On the other, I think a lot about dying lately. I don't get out of bed some days, eat almost nothing, and only muster a little enthusiasm when Gia comes home from school with stories about her day. I live to sleep when my dreams transport me back to Alaska, back to Craig, back to Tony's strong, loving arms. I miss him. I miss him so much, I don't know myself anymore.

But when Elena asked me to come to dinner tonight, I said yes. Partly, because I remembered La Scala from happier days (it was a favorite of my mother's) and partly, because she said that she and Santo would take Gia with them whether I agreed to go or not. I may be depressed as hell, but Gia is still my baby. I wasn't going to let her go anywhere alone with her grandparents.

So here I sit in the back of a beautiful limo, holding Gia's hand, a shell of myself. *This is what happens,* I think, remembering Elena at Giancarlo's funeral. D'Angelo women are worn down by their grief, by their misery, by their disappointment and sorrow. My father was right: the D'Angelos are devils. Nothing but trouble.

Giorgio stops the car in front of the restaurant and Carmine opens Santo's door first. When it slams shut, leaving me alone with Elena and Gia, Elena reaches into her purse and pulls out a thick envelope. She leans forward, shoving it at me.

"Take this," she whispers.

"What is it?"

"Just take it," she says, her voice holding more urgency. "Put it in your purse. Now."

I reach for the envelope, stuffing it into my purse as her door opens. Santo reaches his hand inside, helping her from the car, and leaving Carmine to open Gia's door after her grandmother's been attended to. No one opens mine; a reminder of my place in this family. I slide across the seat, following my daughter out of the car.

"Mamma, we been here before?" asks Gia, looking up at the sign over the front door, which has musical notes rising up from open wine bottles.

"Yeah," I say. "With Nonna and Nonni. The other ones."

"I like it here," she tells me. "They got sundaes for dessert."

I nod at her, following Santo and Elena into the intimate, old-timey restaurant.

Despite the fact that no one smokes anymore, the maroon carpets and dark woodwork hold fifty years of nicotine and smoke in their grains, and I find the smell strangely comforting. Red, diamond-cut glass hurricanes hold flickering candles on every table and waiters hurry around the small dining room in traditional white and maroon uniforms.

The maître-d, Luigi, rushes to greet the D'Angelos, offering his hand to Santo, then kissing the air just above Elena's hand.

"Who is this *principessa*?" he asks, beaming at Gia.

"Our granddaughter," says Elena, placing her hands on Gia's little shoulders. "Say '*Buona Notte*,' *Gia mia*."

My daughter dutifully wishes Luigi a good evening, and he remarks to Santo and Elena that he's never seen a child as beautiful. His eyes rise to mine and he pauses for a second, offering me a half-smile. Realizing that no further introductions will be forthcoming, he quickly returns his attention to Santo.

"I've reserved our best table for you. And our best bottle of *prosecco*," he says, gesturing for us to follow him, "is on me."

"*Grazie, Luigi*," says Santo, pulling out Elena's chair. "*Grazie, vecchio amico*."

"It is my pleasure, *signore*," says Luigi. He snaps his fingers, and four waiters appear behind our chairs to help us with our napkins and pour the sparkling wine. When we each have a half-filled glass, the waiters leave, and Luigi promises to return to take our order in a few minutes.

Santo raises his glass, looking to his right at Elena.

"*Buon anniversario, amore mio*," he says, offering her a smile she doesn't return. "You are my life. You know that. *Salud, Elena*."

Because we aren't included in the toast and it feels like an intimate moment, I don't raise my glass or nudge Gia to do the same.

"You can drink," mutters Santo, gesturing to us. "Drink to my wife. She's a saint, eh?"

"Of course," I whisper, nodding at Gia to do the same.

We each take a small sip of wine, and Gia grimaces from the burn of alcohol and bubbles.

"Puts hair on your chest," says her grandfather.

"I don't want hairs on my chest," Gia tells him.

"Aw, shuddup," says Santo, sighing with annoyance. "I was just kidding."

"Oh," says Gia, lowering her gaze as her eyes shine with fresh tears.

Since New Year's Eve, Gia's been wetting her bed

several nights a week, and I've noticed that tears spring into her eyes almost every time Santo speaks to her. Like me, she's falling apart, but I don't know what to do about it. I can't leave. Anywhere we go, he'll bring us back for Elena. Gia is everything to her grandmother and Santo knows it.

"You," he says, pointing at me. "You're going out with my nephew next week. My brother Vito's kid. It's all set up."

"M-Me?"

"No, her," he says, gesturing to Gia, then chuckling at his own joke. "Yeah, you, dummy. You're gonna go out with him, and maybe you'll make a love connection. Maybe you won't. Who cares? You need a man. Gia needs a dad. After the wedding, you'll both be D'Angelos. Officially. It'll be a good thing."

Indignation flares within me at my life being arranged like this when I'm in love with another man.

I won't do it. I won't fucking do it.

But then I remember Santo's hand hitting my face, and I swallow my words. Instead, I stare miserably at my wineglass, at the tiny bubbles that quickly make their escape to the top only to pop there, trapped in the crystal flute.

"My mamma loves Tony," says Gia. "We *both* love Tony."

"Your mamma will do what I say," says Santo, "if she knows what's good for her... and you."

Gia reaches for my hand under the table and squeezes it. I glance up at her, blinking back my tears and forcing a smile.

"I'm sure Nonni's nephew is really nice, baby," I tell

her. "We'll meet him and find out, okay?"

Gia doesn't say anything; she just pulls her hand away from mine.

"My turn to say something."

I look up in surprise to find Elena holding up her flute of prosecco, a serene, unreadable expression on her face.

"I already said the toast," says Santo. "You don't got to say anything."

"I know that," she says. "But I'd like to."

"Yeah," he says, reaching for his own flute. "Go ahead, *tesora*."

I meet Elena's eyes with mine, and I don't know what I see there, but it sizzles and rolls like fire before she shifts her entire body to face Santo.

"I married you on this day thirty-five years ago," she begins.

"You sure did."

"You swept me off my feet in those days. You were a big talker. A big spender. A beautiful boy," she says, her lips tilting up in a small, sad smile. "You're still good looking, Santo—"

"And you're as gorgeous—"

"But you're not a good person," she says, the smile gone. "Over the course of these thirty-five years, I've lost countless friends… my cousin, Franco… my sister Grace's husband, Jerry, and most recently—" Her voice breaks. Her chest heaves with short, shallow breaths before she is able to continue. "And our s-son. Giancarlo."

Santo is staring at her in shock, his champagne flute still

held aloft.

My mouth has dropped open at some point during her speech and now I close it, though I can't look away as she continues.

"Our arrangement was that you handled the business, and I made us a home. And I fell in line. I turned a blind eye. I enjoyed our big house. My beautiful cars. The vacations to Vegas and Tuscany. I went along with it. With all of it." She pauses for a second, covering her lips with her fingers, and I wonder if she's going to be sick. She closes her eyes and clears her throat. A moment later, she continues speaking. "I went along with all of it until your business killed my baby. My son. My child. My *only* child."

"*Elena mia—*"

"I'm not finished," she growls at him. "Don't speak until I'm finished."

Santo's eyes widen and he raises his chin, but he doesn't argue with her.

"I think I could have stood anything but losing our son. God help me, I could have gone along with *anything* as long as Giancarlo was safe." Her hand begins to shake, and she lowers her glass back down to the table. "But you took him away from me. And from Gia." She looks meaningfully at her granddaughter before sliding hard eyes back to Santo. "She will never know her father because of you." She reaches for her clutch, which sits on the table by her fork, and slides it closer to her. "I know you love me, Santo. But I have no love left in my heart. It's dead. It stopped beating the day our son was killed."

"Elena," says Santo, lowering his glass. "You're not well. We need to go—"

"We're not going anywhere," she says, pulling a small, snub-nosed revolver from her clutch. She points it at Santo, lowers it to her lap, then turns to me.

"Tessa, take Gia to the bathroom. It's by the kitchen."

Shaking like a leaf, I nod jerkily, pushing back my chair and standing up.

"Come on, baby," I say, picking up Gia. I hold her on my hip, and she clings to me tightly; like she knows something very, very bad is about to happen.

I raise my eyes to Elena's. I'm frightened and in shock and scan her face for answers.

"Don't look back," she says softly. "Don't ever look back, *mia care ragazze*."

I nod again, then hurry away, in the direction of the kitchen.

Not a moment later, I hear the *BANG* of a gunshot. Amid the screaming of frightened patrons and employees, I hear another *BANG* a few seconds later. The restaurant erupts into chaos just as I reach the bathrooms, where a young man leans against an old payphone.

"Tessa?" he asks me.

"Yeah."

"Come with me."

"Who are you?" I demand.

"I'm all you've got right now. You can open the envelope in the car. Elena arranged everything."

Reassured by him mentioning Elena's name, I pull Gia

closer and step into rhythm behind him.

Though I know I shouldn't, as we follow the man through the kitchen doors, I glance back to see Elena and Santo D'Angelo slumped over the elegant, round dinner table, their blood turning the crisp white linens as maroon as the carpet.

We follow the man to the back of the kitchen and outside to a waiting town car. He opens the back door for us, then sits down behind the wheel and starts driving.

"Where are we going?" I whisper through tears of shock.

"Newark Airport," he says, glancing at us in the rearview mirror. "Elena said to take you home."

***

Tony

I'm on a job site outside of Klawock, measuring a countertop for a new kitchen sink when my phone pings. A text comes in from a number I don't recognize with a New Jersey area code.

It reads simply:

Tessa and Gia are coming home.

I'm not sure if the message is from Elena D'Angelo or someone else, and for a brief moment, it occurs to me to be wary, but hopefulness overrules caution, and my heart soars. Ever since my puzzling conversation with Elena, during which she seemed to be confirming my commitment to Tessa and Gia, I've been praying for this news. I've been praying that she would do what's best for my girls and send them home to me.

I race to my truck and drive home. I don't know if they're coming via ferry from Ketchikan or airplane to Klawock, so I take a shower and pace back and forth across my living room, glancing at my cell phone every five minutes, and hoping for a follow-up message. Wherever they're coming in, I want to be there to greet them, to hold them, and to bring them home where they belong.

Suddenly, my cell phone buzzes and I scramble to pull it out of my back pocket, entering my passcode as fast as I can.

But there's no text waiting.

Instead, there's a Yahoo! News alert that makes my jaw drop:

Mob Boss Santo D'Angelo And Wife Elena Killed In Newark Murder-Suicide

I suck in a deep breath, staring at the phone in disbelief.

Santo and Elena are dead?

In a murder-suicide?

"What the fuck is going on?" I cry, a chilling thought making my blood run cold:

Did the words "Tessa and Gia are coming home," mean they were coming home to me, or going home to God?

"No, no, no," I murmur like a prayer, clicking on the alert.

My eyes scan the article and I'm shocked to discover that it was Elena D'Angelo who killed her husband and then herself, not the other way around. Apparently, this happened on their anniversary, at La Scala, a high-end Italian restaurant outside of Newark that I used to know well. The story mentions that the D'Angelos arrived at the restaurant with their daughter-in-law and granddaughter, but that neither could be found after the shootings. The police are asking for Ms. Theresa Rinaldi to get in touch with local law enforcement to confirm her safety and shed some light on what happened between Mr. and Mrs. D'Angelo.

"Where are my girls?"

I'm relieved they weren't injured at La Scala, though I'd feel a lot better if I knew where the hell they were.

I sit down on the couch and lower my head, holding my phone between clasped hands.

"Dear God," I pray, my voice broken and soft, "I don't know what happened to Tessa and Gia, but please let them be okay. Let them be safe. Let them be on their way back to me. Please God. I ain't always been the best guy. I've made mistakes. But I'll change. I promise I'll change if you just make sure that Tessa and Gia get here safely. Please, God. I'm begging you. Please."

By the time I finish praying, tears are rolling down my face and I push them away with my palms, searching Yahoo! for more news of the D'Angelo shootings, but unable to find the details I want. A few restaurant patrons mentioned seeing the mother and daughter near the bathroom right before the shootings, but no one at the restaurant seemed to have the slightest idea that anything was amiss before the two fatal shots.

As I'm desperately searching for more information, my phone buzzes again, and I click on my messenger program, my heart pounding as I wait for the message to come up. This one, sent an hour after the first, reads:

They'll be at the airport in Klawock in about an hour.

They're yours now.

Be good to them.

I run upstairs to grab something off my bureau, shrug into my coat, and race to my truck.

It's twenty-five minutes from my house to the airport, so after I park, I have a few minutes to kill before their flight from Juneau touches down. There's no real terminal to speak of, so I sit in my car, my eyes sweeping the sky for a glimpse of their plane. I've had weeks to miss them, to think about them, to figure out what I'd say if they were standing in front of me again. But now that I'm here, I'm nervous. For the first time in my life, I want forever. I just hope that's what Tessa wants too.

To prove my intentions to myself, if not to her, I bought an engagement ring in Florida. At the time, I knew I couldn't give it to Tessa any time soon, but it was important to me to buy it, to have it, to keep it as a symbol of my love for her, and to know that someday—a long time from when I bought it—I'd ask her to be mine forever.

Reaching into my coat pocket, I pull out the black velvet box and stare at it for a second before popping it open. It's a fancy ring—a two-carat solitaire flanked by diamond chips and set in eighteen-karat white gold. I feel like she'll like it. I hope so anyway.

My heart is already hers. All that's left is to see if she wants it.

The *put-put* of a seaplane engine jolts me from my reverie, and I snap the box closed, shoving it in my pocket and opening the car door.

The plane gets closer and closer as I walk toward the landing field, hooking my fingers into the diamonds of the chain-link fence that separates me from the runway. Just before the plane touches down, I catch a glimpse of their faces in the window and my heart soars with joy.

My girls. Home, where they belong.

I wave at the plane but don't move from my place at the fence, standing there in my parka, jeans, and boots, waiting to see them deplane, desperate to welcome them back.

The plane comes to a stop and the little door opens. Stairs are lowered and the pilot steps down onto the tarmac. I strain my neck to get a glimpse of Tessa and Gia, watching as the man offers his hand to someone inside the plane.

Gia, dressed in a bright green dress, puffy black parka, and black boots, deplanes first. My eyes feast on the sight of the best kid in the world, and my face hurts from smiling so hard. I flick my eyes up just in time to see the man help Tessa from the plane. She's also wearing a dress under a black puffy parka, but I can tell from one glance that she's lost weight and I don't like it one bit. My Tessa eats what she likes and likes to eat; if she's lost weight, it's because she's been unhappy.

Well, no more, I think to myself. *You're back home now, baby, and it's my job to keep you happy.*

The pilot gestures to a small terminal building, then

pulls the stairs back into the plane and closes the door. My girls take hands and walk quickly toward the terminal, and I find myself running to meet them, my boots splashing through puddles to get to them.

Just as the terminal doors open, I'm standing in front of them.

And there they are.

Tessa. And Gia. My girls. Mine.

Gia launches herself into my arms and I catch her, feeling her little body tremble with sobs as she buries her face in my neck. I hold on tightly to Gia, but my eyes land on Tessa, who stands back a little, her eyes tired and her face drawn.

"She missed you," she whispers.

"I missed her, too," I say. "And you. God, I missed you so much, Tessa."

She blinks at me, her eyes flooding with tears as she nods. "Me, too."

"I gotta say this before anything else," I tell her, still holding her child in my arms, but stretching out my hand to her. "I love you. Both of you. I love youse so much, it was killing me to be apart. I love youse so much that the only thing keeping me alive was the thought that I'd see you again someday. And here you are. You're home. I almost can't believe it."

She whimpers softly, reaching for my hand and holding it tightly as tears roll down her cheeks.

"I love you, too," she whispers, drawing my hand to her lips.

"Tony loves us, Mamma," says Gia, leaning away from my neck to grin at me, then her mother, then at me again.

"He sure does," I tell her, ruffling her curls as I gently place her down on the ground.

As long as I'm down there, I decide to take a knee. Hell, the ring in my pocket is practically burning a hole. That's the thing about having what you love taken away from you: there's no way you're going to ever let it happen again.

Kneeling before my girls, I reach into my coat and pull out the velvet box. I flip it open and hold it up, grinning at Tessa, who's crying even harder now.

"I promised the woman who answered my ad that I'd offer her paradise and take care of her. I promised walks on the beach and a lifetime of happy memories. Remember?"

She sniffles softly, nodding at me as Gia looks back and forth between us with unmasked delight.

"I remember."

"I say we make today the first memory of thousands. Waddayasay?" I ask her. "Marry me?"

She nods, the motion faster and faster until she's laughing and Gia's laughing and I'm laughing, too. I put the ring on her finger to seal the deal and feel Gia's little arms wrap around my legs as I kiss Tessa.

"Let's go," I say, swinging Gia onto my shoulders.

Tessa puts her hand in mine, and we head home.

Together.

FINAL THOUGHTS

Tessa

There are moments—when I'm watching Tony carry Gia on his shoulders, or when I feel the baby girl growing in my tummy wiggle—that I want to weep for Elena D'Angelo's sacrifice.

In taking *her* life—and Santo's—she gave us *ours* back.

She set us free.

Sometimes, when I dream of her, I remember Tony's rhetorical question about having to choose between a grizzly and a wolf. I imagine Elena as a wolf with her leg caught in a trap.

In her beautiful house with her gorgeous clothes, she was a prisoner who'd lost everything she'd ever loved: her childhood friends, her son, and finally, the chance of a loving relationship with her only grandchild.

There was no way she'd ever escape from Santo, or the miserable life they'd built together. *Or,* I think, *there was* one *escape.*

And she took it.

After Elena and Santo's murder-suicide, the D'Angelo family fell fast.

Vito was murdered days later, his body turning up on the beach in late January. A new family rose to prominence, taking over the turf once run by Santo. There's no more interest in me and Gia. And Antonio Silva's long gone from anyone's memory now.

I like to think that Elena knew what she was doing: knew that in killing her husband and herself, she'd deliver us from evil. I like to think that she did what she did because it was the only way to ensure Gia's—and my—happiness and safety.

I am grateful to her every day—so grateful, in fact, that our baby will be named Angela Elena, after Tony's mother, and Elena D'Angelo, the mother of the boy who fathered Tony's stepdaughter and killed his uncle.

Life sure is weird.

I'm distracted by laughter and look up from my coffee, which I enjoy on the deck every morning, now that the days are sunny and warm again.

Gia sits in a small sailboat at the foot of the dock, wearing a bright orange life jacket over her hot pink flowered bathing suit. Tony waves to me as he steps into the boat beside her, making it rock, which elicits a gale of giggles from my daughter; my precious daughter, who stopped wetting the bed as soon as we returned to Alaska, and finally knows what it is to have a loving father in her life. It's been a ceaseless joy to watch Gia and Tony adopt one another so entirely, and to know that our daughters will grow up with two parents, who love them both to distraction.

Life is wonderful, too, I think, waving back at them.

It's endlessly messy and relentlessly surprising; mind-blowing in its twists and turns, in revealing the unexpected, in shocking reversals of fortune that you couldn't imagine in your wildest dreams.

Life can take the worst situation you've ever encountered and turn it into the gift you never knew you wanted.

I know this better than anyone.

After all, I set out to catfish a cocky stranger and ended up meeting the love of my life.

How's that for a happy ending?

THE END

Odds-Are-Good Stand-Alone Romances

SINGLE IN SITKA – *Available on Amazon + KU*

When Seattle journalist Amanda heads north to Sitka to research a story, she answers the *Odds Are Good* personal ad of single dad Luke, hoping for some no-strings-attached fun. But could the sweet, widowed father of three—who just happens to be a smokin'-hot state trooper—turn out to be the man of her dreams?

NOME-O SEEKS JULIET – *Available on Amazon + KU*

Upon learning that his entry in the Qimmiq Dog Race will be canceled if he doesn't have a female teammate, Cody places an ad in the *Odds Are Good* magazine, desperately searching for a woman in the Lower Forty-Eight to enter the competition with him. Luckily, he recruits Montana-born Juliet, a veterinary student with an agenda of her own.

A FAIRBANKS AFFAIR – *Available on Amazon + KU*

Tired of being treated like a freak when men discover that Faye is a thirty-year-old virgin, she answers an ad in the *Odds Are Good* magazine, hoping to trek up to Fairbanks over New Year's and turn over her v-card to a sexy Alaskan. But when her chemistry with businessman Trevor turns out to be stronger than she ever could have imagined, what started out as a one-and-done mission becomes much more complicated.

MY VALDEZ VALENTINE – *Available on Amazon + KU*

When Los Angeles lawyer Addison receives a desperate voice mail from her adventure-seeking brother, Elliot, she hires Alaskan helicopter pilot Gideon (whom she first discovers via an ad in the *Odds Are Good*) to take her to her brother's last known location. As the two uncover more and more details about Elliot's last days, they find themselves falling deeply for each other.

CATFISHED IN CRAIG – *Thank you for reading!*

ALSO AVAILABLE
from Katy Regnery

a modern fairytale
(A collection)

The Vixen and the Vet
Never Let You Go
Ginger's Heart
Dark Sexy Knight
Don't Speak
Shear Heaven
At First Sight
Love is Never Lost

THE BLUEBERRY LANE SERIES

THE ENGLISH BROTHERS
(Blueberry Lane Books #1–7)

Breaking Up with Barrett
Falling for Fitz
Anyone but Alex
Seduced by Stratton
Wild about Weston
Kiss Me Kate
Marrying Mr. English

THE WINSLOW BROTHERS
(Blueberry Lane Books #8–11)

Bidding on Brooks
Proposing to Preston
Crazy about Cameron
Campaigning for Christopher

THE ROUSSEAUS
(Blueberry Lane Books #12–14)

Jonquils for Jax
Marry Me Mad
J.C. and the Bijoux Jolis

THE STORY SISTERS
(Blueberry Lane Books #15–17)

The Bohemian and the Businessman
The Director and Don Juan
Countdown to Midnight

THE SUMMERHAVEN SERIES

Fighting Irish
Smiling Irish
Loving Irish
Catching Irish

THE ARRANGED DUO

Arrange Me
Arrange Us

ODDS ARE GOOD SERIES

Single in Sitka
Nome-o Seeks Juliet
A Fairbanks Affair
My Valdez Valentine
Catfished in Craig

STAND-ALONE BOOKS:

After We Break
(a stand-alone second-chance romance)

Braveheart
(a stand-alone suspenseful romance)

Frosted
(a stand-alone romance novella for mature readers)

Unloved, a love story
(a stand-alone suspenseful romance)

Under the sweet-romance pen name
Katy Paige

THE LINDSTROMS

Proxy Bride
Missy's Wish
Sweet Hearts
Choose Me
Virtually Mine
Unforgettable You

Under the paranormal pen name
K. P. Kelley

It's You, Book 1
It's You, Book 2

Under the YA pen name
Callie Henry

A Date for Hannah

ABOUT THE AUTHOR

***New York Times* and *USA Today* bestselling author Katy Regnery** started her writing career by enrolling in a short story class in January 2012. One year later, she signed her first contract, and Katy's first novel was published in September 2013.

Several dozen books and three RITA® nominations later, Katy claims authorship of the multititled Blueberry Lane series, the A Modern Fairytale collection, the Summerhaven series, the Arranged duo, and several other stand-alone romances, including the critically acclaimed mainstream fiction novel *Unloved, a love story*.

Katy's books are available in English, French, German, Hebrew, Italian, Polish, Portuguese, and Turkish.